I0622002

PRIME DECEIT

What if the Fountain of Youth Fell Into
the Wrong Hands?

ROBERT A. GORE

To all those grown bone weary of the bullshit.

CONTENTS

ACKNOWLEDGEMENTS

I gratefully acknowledge the powers that be, their cronies, and their minions. They provided such a wealth of material I could manage only to scratch the surface.

CHAPTER 1

METHUSELAHS

Highlights—that was the name of the magazine he had been trying to remember. It was harder to remember things after midnight. It had been his first magazine subscription, when he was a kid in grade school. When it came in the mail, he would flip to the "Hidden Pictures" page. He wouldn't look at the rest of the magazine until he found all the drawing's cleverly hidden-in-plain-sight spools, bananas, candles, toothbrushes, and the like.

Ted Wirth stared at his computer screen, a grown-up Hidden Pictures. Somewhere in the tables, charts, graphs, data plots, bookmarked research monographs, and lecture videos, his browser hid a picture, but he couldn't find it. The computer was slowing up. He had too many applications open—overload. His brain was overloaded, fried. He needed to sleep, to slide into bed with Barbara for a few hours before she went to her shift.

He got up and stuck a K-Cup in the lab's Keurig. He looked in on the Methuselahs as he waited for his coffee. Four mice had lived almost six years, two times the average lab-mouse life-span. Why had they lived so long?

They were severe combined immunodeficiency, or SCID, mice, so named because of a rare chromosomal mutation that prevented their immune systems from working. They were unable to manufacture lymphocytes, a subgroup of disease-fighting white blood cells. In the experiment, human lymphocytes had been transferred to the mice. The mice used the human cells to manufacture their own lymphocytes, which bolstered their immune systems.

Ted stirred powdered creamer into his coffee and returned to his desk. The mice's impaired immune systems made their long lives that much more remarkable...and inexplicable. It was intriguing—or more accurately at one thirty in the morning, maddening—that the Methuselahs had shown no more immune system improvement than other mice in the experiment, which had died months earlier. So their extraordinarily long lives had to be due to something else, but what?

The Methuselahs were unrelated to each other, and genomic analysis revealed no common chromosomal abnormalities. Maybe it wasn't the mice; maybe it was the lymphocytes they received from the humans. On his computer, he clicked on a folder containing the data on the four humans who had "donated" their lymphocytes to the Methuselahs and scrolled through their information forms, their blood-analysis charts, and the histories of where their lymphocytes had gone. Other mice had received lymphocytes from the same donors but were long dead.

Why hadn't he noticed this before? All four of the Methuselahs had been the first to receive the cells after they had been extracted from their respective humans. Could that mean anything?

It could mean many things. Perhaps the Methuselahs had received something before its sell-by date, something that deteriorated quickly. That made no sense, though, because other mice had received their lymphocytes shortly after they were extracted and had not been blessed with abnormally long lives.

Ted ran his fingers through his black, starting-to-gray, starting-to-thin hair and rested his head on the back of his chair. Now that he was forty-two, late nights didn't come as easily as they used to, and he wasn't thinking clearly. High-powered immunological theorizing and exhaustion didn't mix. The combination led to dead ends and pure crap that would be junked the next day. He shut down his computer, gathered up his coat and keys, turned off the lights, and locked the door.

He drove from Sorrento Valley, San Diego's center of medical research, to La Jolla. There were a few cars on Interstate 5, but the surface streets were deserted. He parked his BMW in the apartment building's underground garage. Barbara said she didn't stay up worrying about him coming home late. If she didn't stay up, though, she had to be the world's lightest sleeper. No matter how hard he tried to be quiet, she was always awake, and lately greeting him with a sarcastic comment or two.

He waved his electronic fob before the reader and the door lock clicked. All the lights were off except for the one in the kitchen she kept on so he could see what he was doing. He took off his shoes, tiptoed across the living room rug, gingerly opened the bedroom door, and made his way to the bathroom. After running through his nightly routine, he slipped into bed.

"Any luck on the fountain of youth, Ponce de León?"

"I might have found something, but it was too late, and I was too tired to track it down." He yawned. "Good night."

"Good night."

CHAPTER 2

PRIME HORMONE FACTOR

It was too bad the Jill Yates Foundation had to deal with the government, but the foundation was too big to scoot under the radar. It was doing Important Research, and Important Research could always use a helping hand. Unfortunately, help from the government didn't come without strings: you had to let it know what you were doing with its money. Ted knew the knocks on the conference-room door announced string pullers. He opened the door for his boss, Heather Lindholm, and the two officials from the NIAR.

Lindholm smiled her professional smile. "Ted, I'd like you to meet Dr. Gerald Rawles and Dr. Naomie Cutler, from the National Institute on Aging Research."

Ted shook their hands. "Pleased to meet you."

"We understand you have some very old mice," Cutler said. She was African American, in her midthirties, attractive, well put together. Rawles was twenty years older, higher up in the hierarchy. Ted noticed Cutler's looks; he wouldn't remember Rawles's ten seconds after his departure. *There* was an ugly truth about himself he would have to face someday: he was a typical heterosexual male. Maybe next year.

"Our Methuselahs. Allow me to introduce my colleagues." Ted gestured toward the opposite side of the conference table. "Alan Stafford, Linda Chang, and Terri Gibson are researchers. That's Carl Bartkowski, our lab technician, at the end of the table. You'll be taking those two seats next to Jack Hines, who's also a researcher."

Ted had finally convinced Lindholm—who had in turn convinced her bosses—that the Methuselahs were worth more of an effort than he could devote to them after hours and on weekends. Although one had died, the longer the others lived, the stronger his case became. Ted had gotten four research assistants, a lab tech, and permission to devote his full time to the project. Surprise, surprise—the work had proceeded much more quickly than when it was just his crazy project in the Jill Yates's basement.

"Ted, I'll leave you and your group to explain your exciting research to Dr. Rawles and Dr. Cutler." Lindholm was the most time-efficient person Ted had ever met. There was no way she would sit through a meeting to hear things she already knew, even if the president of the United States were the invited guest.

Ted closed the door, and Rawles and Cutler took their seats.

"Dr. Rawles, Dr. Cutler," Alan said, "can I get you anything to drink? Coffee, or a soda?"

Very good, Alan, make the offer before one of the ladies did. Let our guests know they're in a Full-Equality Space.

Cutler shook her head.

"I'm good," Rawles responded. "And please, it's Gerald and Naomie."

Ted stood to the side of a video screen. Bartkowski clicked a computer mouse, and a real mouse appeared on the screen, one of the Methuselahs. "This is Methuselah two, or M-2, who as of yesterday has lived seventy-nine months, or over eighteen months longer than the longest-lived winner of the Methuselah Mouse Prize."

"There's really a Methuselah Mouse Prize?" Cutler asked.

"Yes, there is, to encourage life-extension therapies in mice. The winner even gets some cash."

"Are you going to submit your mice?"

"After they all die, to see which one sets the record. Moving on." He glanced at Bartkowski, who put up a new screen: bullet points detailing data about the mice's lymphocyte donors and their lymphocytes. Ted took a pointer from the table and pointed at one of the bullet points. "The four do-nors were between the ages of nineteen and twenty-two. Of the donor popu-lation of one thousand nine hundred twenty-seven individuals, there were six hundred sixteen in that age group, or about thirty-two percent. The first working hypothesis was that something in the donated lymphocytes pro-duced the Methuselah effect, but whatever it was, it was only present in less than one percent of the donors in that age group. That led to the hypothesis that perhaps they shared some sort of genomic abnormality or variation, but genomic analysis revealed no such common factor.

"We next asked if there could be something in the lymphocytes, and this proved more rewarding. I won't bore you with all the details…" He bored them with some of the details, ran through the video, took their questions, and concluded his presentation: "It required the full-time chemical-testing and analytic skills of the entire team—much of the work was done in vivo—but we discovered what we are calling the prime hormone factor, or PHF. It may not even be a hormone, but Linda gave it that name, and it stuck."

"It's kind of like the question of whether light is a particle or a wave," Linda explained. "Sometimes it acts like a particle, sometimes like a wave. PHF appears to have an effect on growth and development, which makes it similar to other hormones. However, we've determined that it occurs in minute, almost-undetectable amounts and is unstable once it leaves the do-nor's body. All four of the Methuselahs were the first to receive their donors' lymphocytes. Neither quantities this trace nor the instability is characteristic of hormones, so we cannot say conclusively that PHF is a hormone."

"Have you been able to isolate enough PHF long enough to analyze it?" Rawles asked.

"No. NMR spectroscopy requires more PHF than we've been able to isolate and keep stable," Bartkowski answered.

"Why have you named it the prime hormone factor?"

"That's where this gets exciting, notwithstanding our failure to figure out what it is." Ted smiled. "We went looking for more PHF and found it. Apparently PHF appears in everybody's blood, but only when they're about eighteen to twenty-four years of age, the prime of life. Ergo, the prime hormone. It has some sort of relationship with certain lymphocytes that we don't understand. After one's prime years, PHF disappears, which may explain why it's all downhill from there."

"What is the possibility of synthesizing PHF?"

Well, no mystery why Rawles was working for the government. How did he get through med school? "Synthesis will have to wait until we determine what it is," Ted replied as diplomatically as he knew how. "As it stands now, the only laboratory that can produce PHF is the human body."

"I'm thinking in terms of human life extension. Could PHF be transferred from someone in their prime to someone older, to allow longer life?"

"There are two insurmountable problems with that approach. PHF is in such a trace amount in the human body that to be assured that the recipient got it, the donor's entire blood supply would have to be drained, killing the donor. Also, while a trace amount was sufficient to significantly extend the lives of our mice, it may require much more in humans. It might be proportional to weight. Now maybe our mice didn't receive all of their donors' PHF—they probably didn't. However, for argument's sake, let's assume they did. Taking the average weight of lab mice as eight ounces and the average weight of human recipients as one hundred fifty pounds—which is charitable, given the obesity epidemic—it would take three hundred human transfers, assuming a direct relationship between recipient weight and life extension, to produce in humans the extension shown by the Methuselahs."

The obesity crack was a mistake. Rawles didn't look like he missed any meals.

Rawles nodded. "I see. So our best hope would be synthesis, but at the present time, that's not possible, either."

"No."

"This is certainly fascinating," Cutler said, "but we're going to have to move on and see the foundation's other teams and their projects. Do you have any written materials we could take with us?"

Ted handed them each an orange loose-leaf binder. For some reason, government people liked paper, not flash drives or web links. "That has a page-by-page of the video, and the first draft of a paper we are working on to submit for peer review and publication." Normally the first draft of a paper wouldn't be distributed, but these were the people paying the bills. "Our contact information is also included, should you have further questions. Please feel free to call or e-mail."

"Thank you, Dr. Wirth. Please update us with any further developments."

CHAPTER 3

PATRIOTS

She gazed at him: his alert blue eyes, one covered by a lock of his long brown hair; his narrow, angular face and tanned complexion, marred only by the occasional pimple; the strong line of his jaw. Did she love that face, love him? She didn't know. She did know that she didn't want to hurt him, but she had to do so. There was no easy way to do it.

"What's wrong with you, Aubrey? You've been off somewhere else all night."

She sipped her milk shake, shut her eyes, and shook her head. They were in his Camry at a drive-up hamburger stand. "Connor, there's something I've got to tell you, something you're not going to like."

"Are you breaking up with me?"

"No, not exactly, but there's been a change in plans."

"What are you talking about?"

"I won't be going to IU with you next fall. I'm enlisting in the army."

"What? Are you kidding?"

She looked straight at him. "No, I'm not kidding."

She expected an angry outburst and braced herself for it. He looked away. His long silence, head down, his right fist clenching and unclenching, was far worse, far harder on her, than anger would have been. It became unbearable. "Connor?"

"The army? Why?"

"Because it's the right thing to do. We've grown up here in Plainfield and had a nice life. Our families aren't rich, but we have what we need. It would be great to go to Bloomington with you. But I can't do it. Our country is at war, has been at war, and people like you and me have let others go off and fight for too long. The Muslims—they want to destroy us, and we're all sitting around hoping somebody else will take care of it. If our grandparents had thought like that, we might be speaking German or Japanese today, with no freedom or anything else that we cherish, that makes America great. I know this country isn't perfect, but it's our country, and I'm going to fight for it."

He put his head back on the car seat. "Aubrey...Aubrey, you don't fight for your country. You fight for your government."

"You know, that was clever the first time you said it a couple of years ago, but it's not now. It feels like you're just talking down to me. The government may not be the country, Connor, but it's the people—it's the country's representative and leader. Sure, it's the government who gets in wars and runs the military, but if nobody fights for the government, there might not be any country left. That's why we have government."

"So our government, right or wrong? Fifteen years after 9/11 and we're still in Afghanistan. Al-Qaeda was a small group of crazies in caves back then. Now look at them. We've screwed up in Afghanistan, Iraq, Syria, and Libya, and the Muslims are taking over Europe. Terrorists everywhere because of our damn government. And you want to fight for those clowns? That's not patriotism. That's...that's—"

"That's what, Connor?" she said, her anger rising and her voice with it. "Stupidity? What were we supposed to do after we were attacked? Oh, they're mad because of the Crusades, or imperialism, or something. You've seen the videos. What did those poor people jumping out the towers have to do with any of that? What do you do when you get punched in the face? 'Oh, I'm sorry my face got in the way of your fist. Perhaps when my nose stops bleeding, we can sit down and calmly discuss our differences.' You punch back, Connor! That's your problem. You can't be cool and rational all the time. Sometimes you have to get mad, fighting mad."

"And go around punching people who didn't punch you? What did Saddam Hussein have to do with 9/11? Or Gaddafi? The government didn't like those guys and decided they had to be taken out. They feed us some bullshit, and their defense-company buddies make a lot of money, but it's the soldiers…" His voice dropped. "It's the soldiers who pay the price. They always pay the price, and…and that could be you."

He would never come right out and say it, but he was saying it: He cared for her. He would worry about her. This was hard on him, as she knew it would be. The politics a little, but mostly because of the way he felt about her. Mom said men got angry when they didn't know how to deal with their feelings. Anger was an emotion they could show. He was a great guy, captain of the baseball team, popular, good looking, class vice president, soon to be an honors graduate. They'd been going together since the end of their junior year. The dream couple: she was the class's fair-haired beauty, ran track and cross-country, and would be an honors graduate as well. She cared too much for him to stay angry at him. It was time to cool things down.

"You're entitled to your opinion, Connor. And I'm entitled to mine. I understand how you feel, but don't try to make me feel what I'm doing is stupid or wrong. I don't love our government; sometimes I hate it. But Americans have always defended their country, no matter how they felt about the government."

She put her hand on his cheek. "I'm going to do what I'm going to do, and you know better than to try and stop me. But God I'll miss you. And you'd better miss me, in between your classes and football games and frat parties. We'll talk about it some more, but for now, we're going to agree to disagree. Let's drive over to the park."

The argument was over, or at least postponed. They drove to the park. Making out was always better after an argument, and that night's session was especially torrid: passion spiked with tension, mollified anger, and the impending separation. As he always did, Connor took things only so far and got her home by eleven o'clock, two reasons her parents loved him. Mom would be ecstatic if she married him, but that wasn't going to happen—if it happened at all—until after the army and college.

Holding hands, they walked to the covered front porch of the Elkingtons' two-story home. Her parents gave her time for a few good-night kisses, and then the porch light came on.

"Call me tomorrow after work." She had a weekend job at a clothing store in the local mall.

"Maybe we can get together tomorrow night."

"Mom's going to want to invite you over for dinner, after what I put you through tonight."

"There's definitely some pain, Aubrey." She was surprised he would say that. "But enough about that. I'll call you tomorrow." He kissed her and walked back to his car.

She opened the front door and stepped into the living room, where her parents were watching TV.

"How did it go?" her mother asked.

"Tougher than I thought, but we're still speaking to each other."

"And doing other things." Her father smiled.

"I'm going to bed. Good night."

CHAPTER 4

HIJACKED

Ted and his team, with the exception of Terri Gibson, were in the conference room, seated at a rectangular table, for a meeting with Heather Lindholm, who had not yet arrived. They had no idea what the meeting was about. It was 1:28 p.m., and the meeting was scheduled for 1:30 p.m., but nobody was concerned that Lindholm would be late.

The door opened at 1:30 p.m. Lindholm strode to the head of the table and sat down. Ted found it difficult to read her face, which reflected her stoic personality, but today something was off, out of kilter. Maybe it was the puffiness under her ice-blue eyes, as if she hadn't gotten enough sleep. Ted was annoyed at Terri for being late but wasn't surprised that Lindholm started the meeting without her.

"This meeting will be brief. I'm afraid I have some bad news. The Methuselah project is being terminated. You will not publish anything about the project. In fact, I have to insist that you sign nondisclosure agreements. Officially, it never happened, and any discussion about it after this meeting will be grounds for immediate dismissal. Carl, I need you to ship the three Methuselah mice to NIAR."

The lab technician nodded slowly, perhaps confused but realizing that this was not a time to ask questions.

"Alan, Linda, and Jack, you'll return to the projects you were assigned to before Methuselah."

"What about Terri?" Ted asked.

"With the termination of this project, the foundation's research funding was cut commensurately. Just prior to this meeting, I let her go."

The group was shocked but silent. Ted knew they were dying to question and protest this out-of-the-blue, seemingly arbitrary decision, Terri's dismissal, and the way they were being informed, but Lindholm's face looked as if it were sculpted from granite. Pick your adjective: stern, unyielding, implacable. She looked slowly around the table at each person. It required no great mental acuity to pick up her message: go along or get out. None of them were in a position to make a stand—there were mortgages, car payments, the kids' school tuitions, and grocery bills to pay—although Ted reckoned there might be some résumés going out in that day's e-mails. His might be one of them. This was bizarre. It was beyond bizarre.

"If no one has anything to say, let's get back to work." She stood up and moved quickly toward the door.

"Heather, can I talk with you?" Ted said.

"In my office."

They walked to her office, which was organized and uncluttered, the only decoration an abstract polished-copper sculpture on top of a bookcase. Ted sat in a black leather chair in front of her desk.

"What the hell is going on, Heather?"

"I can't tell you any more than what I just said."

There were people at the foundation who thought Heather Lindholm was a cyborg. Ted knew better. She did not often display her emotions—as per her Scandinavian heritage—but she had them. He had known her three years, and he had learned to recognize subtle stresses and signals. Now, he guessed, the signal was duress, and perhaps an invitation to press on. He would do so. If he was wrong, it wouldn't be the first or last time he misread a woman.

"You can't just shut down a promising project, tell people to keep quiet, fire one of the group, and expect people, or at least me, to go quietly about their business. These are very educated, very bright scientists and technicians, and you can't treat them like children who must unthinkingly obey. It's not fair, and it's unwise. Don't think that these people don't have options, that they'll sit still for this."

He thought she might get mad. What he said could be construed as a threat. Instead, she closed her eyes and took a deep breath.

"Do you know where I was yesterday, Ted?" she said.

He shook his head.

"I was in Oregon, a guest of Jill Yates at her thirty-five-thousand-square-foot mansion. I flew on her private plane, which landed on her private airstrip. Guess who else was on that plane. Alex Galanos. He's been director for nine years, but he told me it was the first time he had been invited to her home. As far as he knew, nobody from the foundation had ever been there; she's very private. Imagine how I felt. Her mansion's entryway is bigger than a good-sized apartment. She was very friendly, gracious. We had lunch. And then she said, 'I'm sure you're wondering why I brought you here to Oregon.' It was like something out of a movie. Of course we were curious."

"So this all came straight from her?"

"All of it. Alex was as shocked as I was. She said that absolute silence was necessary, that this concerned a highly important, very secret matter of national security. We were told in no uncertain terms—actually, we were threatened—that if we said anything about it, we would face unpleasant consequences. That was the word she used—unpleasant."

How could some long-lived mice have national security implications?

"When we got back on the jet, Alex gave me a note saying not to say anything because the jet might be bug—" Lindholm's eyes widened. She put her index finger in front of her lips, signaling silence, reached into the top drawer of her desk, pulled out a pen and message pad, wrote out a message, and slid the pad across the desk.

Don't say anything more. The office might be bugged.

Ted nodded. "Thank you, Heather." He stood, opened the door, walked back to his office, closed the door, leaned back in his desk chair, and stared at the ceiling for a long time.

CHAPTER 5

PENITENCIARÍA

Hector Gomez wiped the sweat streaming down his forehead into his eyes with a dirty rag that left a dark-brown streak. He spit out a green wad, took two green leaves from a plant and cut a slice of lime, put them in his mouth, and started chewing. The coca's pleasant numbness spread from his tongue to his lips and cheeks. His phone rang, and he took it from his front pants packet.

"Hello."

"A raid," a female voice said in Spanish. "Different. Soldiers are with the police. They're everywhere. Helicopters, Hummers, lots of guns. They're not talking to anybody, just arresting everybody. Leave."

"Are they burning fields?"

"No, not yet."

He pressed the off button, confused. A policeman or two he could pay off, but this sounded big. Soldiers meant a federal force. Politicians had promised to eliminate coca for decades, but everyone knew they made too much money from bribes to ever stop it. The only way it would stop was if all the Americans quit using it—never.

He gathered his tools and dropped them in a canvas bag. The plants— what if they burned his field? There was nothing he could do about that, but it was so close to harvest. It would be a huge blow. Worse, if they spread chemicals, the land would be useless. He'd have to clear the rain forest. Even with his sons helping him, that was an effort he would not want to make.

His bag and canteen slung over his shoulder, he jogged awkwardly through the six-foot coca plants. Despite his hurry, he still noticed the leaves—just turning yellow—that had holes from the caterpillars. For most pests, coca was its own pesticide. It didn't, however, stop the small green coca caterpillars. They were as big a threat as the government; their appetite for shoots and leaves destroyed entire plants.

Gomez reached the edge of the coca field and ran across a narrow, open strip into the rain forest. The tall trees' branches blocked the sun. Anyone who did not know the way would soon be lost. The forest was on the foothills of the Andes, and Gomez puffed and sweated profusely running up the slope. The pitch became more pronounced as he neared his destination, the cave.

Only a small child could have discovered the cave behind the boulders. The crack between the boulders was too small for anyone else to squeeze through. What that small child had found on the other side was a crawl space leading to a cave large enough to hold at least twenty men. It even had a stream running through it. Someone, probably the child's father, had enlarged the hole sufficiently so that he could enter, and realized that the cave was a perfect sanctuary.

The cave was a closely guarded secret. Most of the adult population of Hector's village—and many children—were engaged in either the cultivation or processing of coca. A painful death was the fate of anyone known to have revealed anything about the cave, even if the revelation was only an inadvertent admission that it existed. It offered the men important to the village's coca production their last refuge in case of raids by the government or criminal gangs (often one and the same) that could not be paid off or defeated. It was a village rite of passage: male youths deemed trustworthy were shown the location of the cave. Women, deemed expendable, had no access.

Hector reached the top of a ridge above the bowl-like depression where carefully arranged rocks hid the cave's entrance. Police and soldiers—they saw him! There were at least twenty of them, some on horseback. He turned and ran but was no match for the men on horses. The police and soldiers did not shoot, the usual response to flight. They surrounded him, pointing their rifles and pistols. He raised his hands in surrender. One of the policemen dismounted from his horse and approached him, pointing his pistol at him.

"You're under arrest. Drop to your knees and put your hands behind your back."

He did as instructed. Handcuffs were secured around his wrists.

"Get up."

He did so, expecting a blow from a nightstick. That was the usual way of softening a prisoner up, but there were no blows. Instead, the arresting officer pointed with his nightstick in the direction of the cave.

"This way."

The men on horseback rode away, and the rest of the little group followed them. They did not stop when they reached the cave, but kept walking for about a mile to a small clearing where thirty or forty soldiers and policemen stood guard over twelve prisoners, all with their hands in cuffs behind their backs. Hector recognized the prisoners; they were all from his village. He said nothing to them, betraying no recognition that the police and military could use against him or them.

For the next ninety minutes, the men stood quietly as other men were brought in, until there were nineteen in the group. A military officer shouted, "March!" and the group followed the soldiers away from the clearing through the rain forest. Hector could tell from the occasional glimpses he caught of the sun through the forest canopy that they were heading west, away from his coca field and the village. They walked for over an hour, the prisoners' journey painful because of the uncomfortable position of their arms behind their backs and the handcuffs biting into their wrists. Eventually they reached a large field with a dirt road running next to it. There was a line of green troop-transport trucks, some with *US ARMY* stamped in black on their sides.

The prisoners were marched to the trucks. There were other prisoners on some of the vehicles. A soldier came up behind Hector and roughly blindfolded him, cinching the knot tightly behind his head. Grabbing his arm, the soldier led him up a plank to the bed of one of the trucks and shoved him down on a wooden bench seat, where he was wedged tightly between two other prisoners. After about thirty minutes, the truck started to move, jostling the prisoners against each other as it ran over the rutted road. Dust filled the truck. Hector was parched, but having no idea who was in the back of truck with him, he said nothing. A policeman or soldier might club him for complaining.

The ride was several hours—Hector guessed four or five—of hell. The truck's lurching and swaying, the sweat and farts of the prisoners so tightly packed together, and the heat, dust, and humidity made him sick to his stomach. The dust dried out his mouth, nose, and throat. They were not given water, and there was no way he could get to the canteen hanging by a leather strap on his shoulder. It was odd that a man could be thirsty and have to pee at the same time, but he found himself in that unpleasant state, his discomfort further compounded by a need to shit.

Only the truck leaving the rough dirt road for a smooth paved one gave him any relief. They were on that road for about ten minutes before they came to a stop. The truck moved a length or two, jerked, stopped, moved again. Hector guessed they had come to a checkpoint. After a stop, he heard the truck driver talking to a man he assumed was a guard.

"How many prisoners?"

"Nineteen."

"Just follow the other trucks. You'll be parked in rows in the yard."

They drove a short distance, made a turn, drove another short distance, made another turn, slowed, maneuvered back and forth, and came to a stop.

"Stand up," a voice ordered. The prisoners stood. Hector heard the gate at the back of the truck being unlatched and lowered. He heard planks being lowered from the gate to the ground. The prisoners shuffled down the planks. After Hector stepped off, a voice said, "Stop!" and Hector's blindfold was removed.

They were in a large dirt field. A huge, windowless gray cement building with many floors stood on one side, and a smaller, but still large, two-story, freshly painted white stucco building stood on the other. Parked in the yard were at least fifty troop transports. Prisoners, all handcuffed, were being marched from the trucks and arranged into rows. In front of them stood a military officer holding a megaphone. After standing for a few minutes, Hector and the other men from his truck were led by a guard to their places in a row. Eventually the trucks were emptied, and all the prisoners were in formation.

"I am General Cardenas," came the voice from the megaphone, "the commandant of this facility. You have been arrested as part of the biggest crackdown on narcotics and terrorism in our nation's history. We will break the backs of both. Only a small group of officials is aware of this facility. Other than that group, nobody knows you are here, so nobody will find you. By sweeping you all up at once and bringing you here in secret at the same time, we make sure that this investigation will not be ruined by traitor informants, bribery, and escapes, like so many have been ruined in the past."

Cardenas paced back and forth and gestured with his megaphone toward the gray building. "After we have obtained your names and identification cards and inventoried your papers and possessions, you will be taken to that building, where you will be put in your cells. You will receive three meals a day. In the interior of the building is a courtyard. Prisoners who maintain good behavior will be given access to it twice a day for exercise and communication with other prisoners. You will be subject to judicial process in the jurisdiction in which you were arrested. Starting tomorrow morning you will each undergo routine medical screening in the building behind me."

The general stopped pacing. "A word of caution to any of you who may be thinking of escape. You are only seeing a small part of this facility. It is surrounded by a three-meter electrified fence with coiled razor wire at the top, and there are computer-monitored infrared sensors. There are eight guard towers, manned by at least four guards at all times. The towers have spotlights that sweep the grounds all night. The guards are under orders to shoot to kill, without warning, anyone who approaches the fence without authorization. All vehicles are searched when they enter and exit. Your cells will be searched randomly, without notice. Bribery will be out of the question. All money you have will be confiscated and returned only when you leave, including any found during the cavity search that will be part of the medical procedure. Any prisoner caught trying to escape who is not shot will wish he had been. He will be in solitary confinement in a very small cell for the duration of his time here. That is all. Please stay in the rows you are in. You will be individually processed."

At the end of each row, guards set up portable tables and placed clipboards with papers, fingerprint scanners, ink pads, stamps, cameras, and laptop computers on them. Hector had been arrested before and spent time in jails, but he had never seen anything like this. There were two guards behind each desk, but it took at least five minutes to process each prisoner. It was over an hour before Hector reached the table for his row. At the table his handcuffs were removed from his sore wrists.

"Name?"

"Hector Gomez."

"You have your identification card?" Hector removed the card from his wallet, and the guard attached it to a sheet of paper with a paper clip. "Date of birth?"

"August 19, 1960."

"Place of birth?"

"Santa Rosa."

The guard asked Hector many questions and typed the answers into a computer. When he was done with the questions, he took Hector's picture and electronically scanned his fingerprints. Both the camera and the scanner were attached to the computer. Hector assumed it stored his picture and prints.

When he was done with the processing, a guard led him to the gray concrete building. It was both better and worse than the jail cells he had been in previously. He had his own cell, and it was spotless, as if it had never been used. Cellmates could be good or bad, but they were at least someone to talk with. The back wall was cement; the other three walls were steel. He would be unable to communicate with his neighbors through the walls, which he had done at other jails. The lighting was good, and there was a small metal table with books and magazines, something he had never seen before in a cell. The mattress on his steel-frame cot was reasonably firm, not lumpy, and did not smell of fumigant. There was a neatly folded stack of prison clothes, all olive green: two shirts, pants with an elasticized waist, two pairs of socks, and underwear. Another departure—the steel toilet gleamed and did not smell, and the flusher handle worked.

Hector, who had spent most of his adult life on the edge of the law, suddenly felt more frightened than he had ever felt before. His sterile cell and the isolation, quiet, and order oppressed him. It wasn't as if he were even in jail; it was much worse, a tomb. Though it was unwise to speak to a guard you didn't know, he couldn't stop himself.

"How long will I be here?"

The guard had a long face, with jowls drooping like a hound's, and brown eyes that were not unsympathetic and hard, as guards' eyes usually were. "If I knew, *señor*, I would tell you, but I do not know." He closed the cell door with a soft clang.

Time was different in jail. It didn't flow from one event to another. Being in jail was like drifting on a river so wide and placid, through jungle so thick, there was no sensation of movement, no expectation, no anticipation. Occasionally you drifted into some change of scenery, but it would be brief and inconsequential and soon would give way to slow drift through more of the same. Jail was beyond patience, which implies being patient for something. It was resignation: there was no reason to look forward. Some did, to the meals or the showers or the time in the yard, but that was dangerous because the warden and the guards could inflict agony just by varying the routine a little.

He picked up a magazine and plopped down on the cot. He glanced around his cell. No cameras. Good, at least he'd be able to pull Pedro.

CHAPTER 6

SYRIA

Boot camp had been rough, especially physical training, PT. There were a few Amazons who had upper-body strength to match the men, but most of the women didn't. Aubrey had been on the cross-country and track teams. She had the stamina and endurance for marching, hiking, and running, but the arm, chest, and shoulder muscles that were unwanted back in high school—just more weight to carry—would have come in handy. The weight lifting and strength exercises she had done before basic hadn't been near enough for PT.

She wasn't as strong as most of the men, but if test scores and class performance were any indication, she was smarter than just about all of them, and today's army was a high-tech, high-brain-power enterprise. Smiling, she copied to her notepad the trajectory formula the instructor had just written on the blackboard. It was not technically necessary to know the formula; a computer given the proper inputs would solve the equation. But as far back as she could remember, it had never been enough just to get the right answers; she had always wanted to understand why she got the answers she did. Now, it was not enough to know what the dials, lights, indicators, and switches on the tactical data systems were for; she wanted to know how the systems actually worked, the principles on which they operated. Her hand went up more than anyone else's in her classes, annoying the bad instructors, delighting the good ones.

In less than two weeks, she would be done with her seven-week Advanced Individual Training as a *field artillery automated tactical data-systems specialist*. What a mouthful of a Military Occupational Specialty. There had been times during basic training when she thought she wasn't going to make it. She was happy she had stuck it out. AIT was completely different from basic—much more classroom and specialized training, much less PT. Data systems were interesting and could put her in high-pressure, high-stress combat situations, but not right on the front lines. The training she was receiving now, and the experience she would gain, especially if she deployed to a war zone, would make her quite employable after she got out of the army and college.

The ten weeks of basic had been the longest she had ever been away from her family. Her mother, her father, her two little sisters, and Connor came to Fort Sill the day before graduation. Although she had a nasty cold, it was great seeing her family, hanging around with them. It was not so great seeing Connor. There she was, with hundreds of athletic, good-looking men in prime physical condition. He must have realized that their relationship was probably not going to survive her tour of duty. She had made no protestations of undying love, freely admitting to herself, but not to him, that there were times at basic she would have jumped in the sack with the first hard body that crooked his finger. But come on, it wasn't going to be any different for him. He had those dark good looks and piercing blue eyes. There would be no shortage of hot and horny babes at IU. She'd be a memory after his first hookup.

Several times a day she asked herself the all-consuming question, where would she be deployed? There was supposedly a shortage of artillery data-systems specialists. If true, she might be sent to the Middle East or Afghanistan. That possibility intrigued and frightened her. Well, maybe not frightened, but definitely caused some nervous butterflies, more intense than what she used to have before cross-country and track meets. Nervous or not, she would rather go to the Middle East than be stuck on a base somewhere and see no action. She was in the army to fight for her country, not to play soldier, see the sights, and collect her college tuition. There were some who were here on the easy-rider plan, but that wasn't her.

Aubrey's deployment order came a week later. A conflict had waxed and waned in Syria and Iraq for the better part of three years. It was the typical Middle Eastern fracas: hapless governments and their armies; not-so-hapless sectarian brigades with colorful names waging guerrilla war, detonating bombs, promoting mayhem; shifting alliances; endless intrigue; diabolical duplicity; rampant disinformation; appearances masking antipodal realities; and machinations by outside string pullers, money honeys, and intelligence agencies who never seemed to realize—or if they did, never acknowledged—that they were the puppets, not the puppeteers. Despite the seeming complexity, the war boiled down to the usual two issues: oil and the centuries-old question of Muhammad's rightful heir.

Governments couldn't resist throwing matches on the gasoline. Sunni nations—Turkey, Saudi Arabia, and the rich little monarchies scattered around the Persian Gulf—as well as a variety of sectarian brigades with colorful names, launched massive and coordinated maneuvers to "restore order" (Middle Eastern–speak for replacing a government with one more to your liking) to Shiite Syria and Iraq. The Shiite governments were not without friends. Russia, Iran, and various sectarian brigades with colorful names would not let them go down without a fight. So in a very short time, the corner of the world with the highest per capita concentrations of troops, terrorism, weapons, and warfare saw exponential increases in all four.

The US government urged all parties to come to the negotiating table. No parties came to the negotiating table. The US government consulted with its European allies. A resolution was submitted at the United Nations. The war intensified. The war lobby screamed: this was World War III, and the United States was not there! It was like missing your senior prom! The Europeans screamed. Refugees were streaming to Europe. Despite welcoming gestures, the only assimilating they seemed to be doing was slurping up government benefits. It was getting expensive. Some Europeans didn't like their new guests. Some of their new guests didn't like the Europeans, but they did like blowing people up. Voters were getting mad. Something had to be done!

The US government ultimately did what the US government does best: came up with a catchy name (Operation Restoration of Peace, Freedom, Hope, Democracy, and Dignity in the Middle East), parked aircraft carriers in the Mediterranean and Persian Gulf, dropped bombs, and deployed thousands of troops to "advise and assist" without a clear idea of whom they would be advising and assisting. It implored the Europeans to join its efforts, to staunch the refugee flow by making war, blowing things up, and creating more refugees. Back in the States, the groups that reflexively cheered every war distributed more *Support Our Troops* bumper stickers.

Two months and one day after completing her AIT, Aubrey found herself with 187 other soldiers on a Boeing C-17 transport bound for Incirlik, Turkey, discussing their pending engagement.

"Anybody know where we're going from Turkey?"

"Nobody knows that, not even the brass. They're making this shit up as they go along."

"You look on a map, and we won't be far from Syria, but Iraq is just down the road, too."

"So we're going to Syria or Iraq. You're a fucking genius."

"Who we fighting?"

"Mooslims."

"They're all Muslims."

"Well, there are peaceful, God-fearing Mooslims—regular Christians— that love the United States and all it represents, and there are bad Mooslims. We'll be fighting the bad ones."

"How do you tell the good from the bad?"

"Jake's full of shit. There's no good ones. They're all fucking terrorists; they all hate us. Shoot first and ask questions later."

"Is Turkey Mooslim?"

The soldiers looked at Aubrey. They had noticed, when they weren't staring at her tits and ass, that she was well informed. "Yes, Turkey's Sunni Muslim." For the most part she was spared the hazing and abuse that were routine among the male soldiers. Some of them wanted to get into her pants.

"They must be good Mooslims if they let us fly into their country."

"So don't shoot any of them while we're in Turkey."

"Is Syria Sunni or Shiite?"

"Syria is majority Sunni," Aubrey said, "but the government is run by a Shiite sect. That's why Turkey and the other Sunni countries, Saudi Arabia and the Gulf states, don't like Syria. Iraq and Iran are Shiite."

"But Russia's lined up with the Syrian government. Are we going to fight them as well as Mooslims?"

"No, Russia sometimes treats the groups the United States is supporting like they were terrorists because they're trying to overthrow the Syrian government, but we're both supposed to be fighting terrorists."

"So don't shoot at any Russkies unless they shoot at you first, but even then, try to dialogue with them to see if it's just a simple misunderstanding, or this whole thing could go nuclear."

The C-17 tilted downward as it began its descent. Back in civilian life, Aubrey usually took the window seat so she could look out and see the terrain when her plane landed. There were no windows in the bay of the C-17. The soldiers sat in sidewall seats and nine seat pallets in the center of the bay. On its next flight, instead of soldiers the versatile C-17 might haul tanks, other vehicles, helicopters, or cargo pallets.

It made a smooth landing and taxied to a stop. Because the plane would be immediately reloaded with passengers or cargo after the soldiers deplaned, the engines were not shut off. The troops had been briefed earlier on off-load procedures while the engines were running. Aubrey took one of her two pairs of standard-issue earplugs from a pocket on her shirt and inserted them into her ears.

Hydraulic cylinders raised the rear cargo door and lowered the ramp. The soldiers unbuckled their seat belts, stood, checked themselves for loose clothing and other items that could potentially get sucked up into the engines, formed orderly lines, and began their exit. Even with the earplugs, the engines were loud. It was dark outside, cloudy with few stars visible, but not raining, and the off-load personnel wore reflective orange vests and belts. The soldiers stepped single file down the ramp and were directed twenty-five yards behind the C-17, there to veer off to the left. They walked about a hundred yards to four buses, indistinguishable from school buses except they were army green instead of yellow-orange. The buses took them to a group of barracks where they would spend their first night in Turkey.

⋏

Aubrey got her orders three days after her arrival. She would advise and assist Syrian rebels who had just received American artillery and associated control systems. With the US escalation, battle-tested artillery data-systems specialists were in short supply. Only specialists fresh from AIT could be spared for training United States' allies.

Incirlik was a noisy hub of activity with aircraft ranging from helicopters to fighter jets flying in and out twenty-four hours a day. At dawn the day after she received her orders, she boarded a Chinook transport helicopter with forty members of her battery, including two other novice data-systems specialists. The helicopter was part of a convoy taking troops, supplies, and light artillery to a location in northeastern Syria near a Kurdish stronghold.

Aubrey looked out a window at a brown, beige, and barren landscape below. "We've been in the air over an hour, which means that's Syria down there," she said to Roger, the soldier sitting next to her.

He leaned over her to look out the window. "I don't see all hell breaking loose."

"Well, if it was, we wouldn't be flying over it in helicopters."

He smiled. He had a nice smile and an interesting, chiseled face. Boot camp did good things to men's faces, tightened 'em up. "Kind of odd how the Turks and Kurds hate each other, but they're both supposedly US allies," he said.

"The Middle East is full of odd. It's tough for outsiders to get a grip on it."

"Maybe that's why we haven't done so well over here."

"I'm sure that's part of it."

"You're one of the smart ones."

"How do you know that?" She smiled.

"Let's just say I'm observant. Did you read up before you were deployed?"

"Did you?"

"Yes."

"Well, so did I."

For the next hour, she talked with Roger about the Middle East. He was smart and well informed, had a sense of humor, and obviously enjoyed the conversation. The helicopters began to land at different sites. Aubrey's helicopter touched down in a dusty patch of dirt next to a fortified US forward operating base, Wolverine. The three remaining helicopters headed east. The soldiers disembarked and walked with their packs and rifles to Wolverine.

The US Army probably had more experience erecting temporary outposts in a hurry than any other institution in the world, and FOB Wolverine was a monument to the Corps of Engineers' skills. In what Aubrey assumed was a short time, a rectangular army camp had sprung up in the desert, complete with barracks, a cafeteria, large tents, portable toilets, watchtowers in the corners, two gates, and a barbed wire fence. Many of the buildings were protected by HESCO bastions: sand-filled gabions stacked two units high that afforded some protection against artillery and rifle fire. They were a reminder, if one was needed, that the soldiers were now in a war zone. To the south it was flat and brown; to the northwest and northeast were hills and greenery.

Aubrey was told at the gate where she checked in that lunch would be at 1140 and after lunch she was to report to tent D. That gave her and the other soldiers on the helicopter about forty minutes to "explore" Wolverine, an exploration that took no more than ten. The outpost was functional, Spartan, and, coupled with the monotonous landscape, uninteresting. They had their lunch in the cafeteria, and Aubrey reported to tent D with Bill and Dave, two data-systems specialists. She knew Dave from AIT at Fort Sill.

Inside the tent were consoles and hardware, the components for various data systems, a dry-erase board with markers, two tables, and ten chairs. A major stood in front of the dry-erase board.

"Welcome to expedited field artillery automated tactical data-systems specialist school. I'm Major Sanders. A few months ago you were students; in a few hours you'll be teachers. You'll each be individually training a member of the Syrian New Dawn Fighters for Islamic Justice, a rebel group that shares America's antipathy for Syria's present ruler but which is characterized as moderate. Over here 'moderate' means they line up their enemies, including women and children, and shoot them instead of beheading them. I have been assured that the three Syrians we are training are technically proficient and have a reasonable degree of fluency in English. I'll believe it when I hear it. This session will be three and a half hours. After today, there will be two sessions a day for the next eight days. So you are expected to teach them in nine days what it took you seven weeks to learn. Let it be a challenge. I thought a little review before the Syrians arrived would be in order."

For the next two hours, they brushed up on the data systems and the conditions under which they would be used in the field. The first few sessions would be held in the tent, but there would also be field training. Aubrey had not forgotten much since AIT and felt fairly confident she could teach her Syrian pupil.

A jeep drove up carrying three Syrian men. They wore military-style boots and carried AR-15s, but other than that, they were irregularly dressed in faded and torn jeans and camouflage jackets. They jumped out of the jeep and strode into the tent, examining their surroundings and the equipment. Even at a distance Aubrey caught the stench of men who hadn't bathed in weeks, maybe months. She should get hazardous-duty pay for this mission.

Major Sanders looked at a card on the table. "Which one of you is Anas?" Anas stepped forward. "And Sayid?" Sayid stepped forward. "So you must be Rifat." Rifat nodded.

"I'm Major Sanders. This is Private Danbury, Private Mills, and Private Elkington. Anas, you'll train with Private Danbury, Sayid with Private Mills, and Rifat with Private Elkington."

Rifat stared at Aubrey as if she were a cartoon blaspheming Muhammad. Pretty, blond, blue eyes, and a female soldier among males: probably all blasphemies. He gesticulated wildly and unloosed a torrent of angry-sounding Arabic. She glanced at Major Sanders.

"He's saying welcome to Syria, and he's looking forward to working with you."

CHAPTER 7

THE PROCEDURE

"Where are the younger men?" Santos whispered.

Hector shook his head. He didn't know, none of the older prisoners did, and the guards wouldn't say. Every day he and the rest of the older prisoners, about sixty men, took their meals together in the cafeteria, exercised in the yard, and showered in the communal facility, but they never saw the younger prisoners, a far larger group.

"And why haven't we been brought before a court?"

Hector again shook his head. Santos was always asking questions he knew nobody could answer. Why did he do that? They were in the yard, sitting on the asphalt surface with their backs against the wall. The walls had ears, as the saying went, so why say something that could get you in trouble when you knew you would learn nothing?

"It smells like rain," Hector said. "Clouds are moving in." He pointed toward the sun, now obscured behind those clouds.

"Why did they do all those medical tests?"

That was it. Hector stood. "I'm going to walk around, stretch my legs." He didn't like Santos much, and the questions were annoying, perhaps because they were the same questions Hector asked himself. He walked to the other side of the rectangular courtyard, surrounded by the four walls of their building, and paced around the perimeter.

Why *did* they do all those tests? The morning of the second day after his arrival, there had been a knock on his cell door and two guards entered. They escorted him to a shower, not the communal one but a single shower, with plenty of soap, shampoo, and hot water, and told him to wash thoroughly. He didn't need to be told twice. Good showers had been a rare luxury in his harsh life.

He took his shower and was given a clean set of the prison's olive-green clothes. The two guards escorted him out of the prison building and across the dirt field where he had been processed on his first day. They entered the white stucco medical facility. A guard behind a desk, reading from a paper on his clipboard, verified Hector's name, birth date, and place of birth, where he lived when he was arrested, and the other information he had given them. After the guard had run through his checklist, he issued Hector a wristband, helped him put it on, and cut off the excess part with scissors. Then something very odd happened.

A guard took him to a brightly lit room with stark white walls. The only furniture was a blue plastic chair. The guard told him to take off all his clothes. He left and Hector stripped, putting his clothes on the chair. A middle-aged man in civilian clothes entered the room carrying a camera.

"*Buenos días, señor.*" He sounded like an American speaking Spanish. "I'm going to take pictures. Follow my instructions." Definitely an American. With that, he began taking pictures, many pictures, of Hector's face and body, occasionally telling him to spread his legs, raise his arms, and so on. The photographer took pictures from many angles of Hector's face and every part of his body, even the bottoms of his feet and top of his head. When he was done, he told Hector to put his clothes back on, said "*gracias*" as if he had done nothing out of the ordinary, and left the room.

Hector put his clothes back on. A guard came and escorted him to a large room, a medical lab with many instruments and machines. He would spend the next seven hours in that lab: giving blood, spit, urine, hair, and shit samples to English-speaking Americans (a bilingual guard was the translator) who wore green outfits and white masks over their mouths and noses and were always washing their hands; submitting to tests, x-rays, scans, and the cavity search the commandant had promised; walking, then running, on a treadmill and riding on a stationary bicycle while machines with wires clamped to metal plugs taped to his skin monitored his heart rate, breathing, and other information, all of which was displayed on screens and recorded on computers. Hector had been born in his mother and father's bedroom and had been in a hospital only once—to have a broken leg set and put in a cast when he was sixteen. He had not even gone back to get the cast removed, sawing it off himself after six weeks. This lab was as far removed from his experience as a trip to the moon.

The lab workers finished their tests and procedures without offering any explanation for what they had done. Hector didn't ask. Two guards escorted him from the medical building. It was raining, and they ran across the muddy field.

The medical examination had been a week ago. Hector had learned that all of the other older prisoners had undergone similar examinations. They let you die in most prisons. Medical care was dispensed from dirty one-room infirmaries by staff doctors and nurses indifferent to the fates of their patients. If you died, as prisoners grimly joked, it saved the government the expense of taking care of you. This was the strangest prison he had ever seen. And why were most, if not all, of the workers in the medical lab Americans? Nothing made sense.

A guard approached him. "Your time in the yard will be over in a few minutes. Instead of going to the cafeteria for lunch with the rest of the prisoners, you will return to your cell."

"When will I eat?"

"You will not be eating. You will be fasting. We will bring you water in your cell. That is all you may have."

"How long will I be fasting?"

"Until we decide to feed you, understand?"

Hector nodded. Were they going to starve him? Why would they do all those tests if they meant to starve him? Nothing made sense here. Nothing.

A few minutes later, the guard who had told him he was fasting led him back to his cell. The guard left and returned shortly with a plastic bottle full of water and a plastic cup. "You will not be taking dinner tonight," he said before he shut the cell's door. It had a harsh sound, a metallic clang of finality.

⚓

Early the next morning, Hector was awakened by a guard's knock on the door and escorted to an individual shower, as he had been the day of the medical examination. After he showered and put on a clean set of clothes, two guards took him to the medical building. A guard verified his information, and another guard led him to a room with a gurney under a high-intensity lamp. Next to the gurney were a machine with plastic bags and tubing and another machine with an instrument panel. There was a blue plastic chair in the corner. Shortly after the guard left, a nurse came in carrying a hospital gown.

"¿Habla usted Inglés?"

Hector nodded.

"Take off your clothes, except your underwear, and put this on. The slit goes in back. There are ties in the center and at the top. I'll be back in a few minutes. If you have trouble with the ties, I'll tie them when I get back."

He had to put on this stupid gown! "What is happening?"

"They discovered a blood abnormality when they ran your tests. It could make you very sick, so they are going to do a procedure that will prevent that."

"A abnormalty?"

"Abnormality. You'll be under sedation when the procedure is performed."

"Sedation?"

"You'll be asleep. The procedure will be painless. In fact, you should feel better afterward. The doctor will explain it to you." The nurse left.

Hector took off his clothes and put on the hospital gown, feeling like a fool. He couldn't tie the ties and felt more foolish when the nurse came back and tied them for him.

"If you'll just sit here," the nurse said, motioning toward the gurney. "I need to get your blood pressure and some other information, Mr...."—he checked a paper on the clipboard he was carrying—"Gomez."

Hector sat on the gurney, and the nurse took his blood pressure and temperature, measured his respiration and pulse, and wrote numbers on his clipboard. He placed Hector's finger in a plastic clamp attached to a wire running from the machine with the instrument panel. He waited a few minutes, then copied numbers from a display. "Thank you, Mr. Gomez. I'll be back in a few minutes with the doctor, and we'll begin the procedure."

A few minutes turned out to be over half an hour. Still sleepy from his early morning wake-up, Hector turned off the bright overhead light, stretched out on the gurney, and took a nap. He awoke and sat up when the nurse came in with a doctor.

"Mr. Gomez, I'm Dr. Harris. I'll be performing today's procedure."

"Why is everybody here American?"

"We're funded by the US government. The state of medical care in your prisons is not what it should be, and your government asked for our government's help. The tests you underwent last week were so that we could get a complete picture of your health. Unfortunately—or actually, fortunately—we discovered a condition in your blood that requires today's procedure. This is relatively minor, and you'll be in no danger at all."

"I'm going to give you a sedative, Mr. Gomez," the nurse said. "I'm also going to put a needle in your arm. The needle will be attached to a tube for anesthesia. Do you know what anesthesia is?"

Hector shook his head.

"It will put you to sleep during the procedure. If you didn't have it, you would experience some pain."

Hector was nervous about being put to sleep. Would he wake up? But why go to all this trouble if all they were going to do was kill him? They could have shot him at any time since he arrived—one bullet and much less fuss.

The nurse gave him a pill and a paper cup of water. Hector took the pill. The nurse tightly wrapped a rubber tube around Hector's left arm. His veins bulged below the tube. The nurse stuck a needle with a metal valve at the end of it into a forearm vein.

"Mr. Gomez, would you please lie down?"

Within a few minutes, Hector felt himself relaxing, his fears fading. The nurse was saying something and wheeling him down a brightly lit hallway. Double doors opened automatically, and he was wheeled into a big room with several high-intensity lamps. A doctor, not the one he talked to in the other room, screwed a tube into the valve on his arm. That was the last thing he remembered.

⋏

When he woke up, back in the first room he had been in that day, Hector had no idea how much time had passed. He was hooked up to several machines and felt lightheaded, dizzy. What happened now? When would he go back to his cell? Thinking was an effort. He lifted the sheet that covered his body. The nurse had only put a needle in his left arm, but now he had bandages on both arms. Had they put a needle in his right arm, too?

The nurse came in about ten minutes later.

"What happened to this arm?" He lifted his right arm.

"We needed to administer more anesthesia, and it's safer to put it into both arms at a lower rate than to use just one arm at a higher rate."

He nodded as if he understood, but he didn't. Something did not seem quite right, but it was hard to think about this, or anything else, right now.

"You'll feel better as the anesthesia clears your system. We're going to take some measurements, and the doctor will be examining you. Then you'll go back to your cell."

The doctor came in twenty minutes later. He studied the monitors on the machines and told the nurse to disconnect Hector from them.

"Mr. Gomez, would you please sit up and take off your hospital gown?"

Hector did as instructed. The doctor examined him, putting a stick on his tongue, shining lights in his eyes, ears, and mouth, banging his knee with a little hammer, and listening to his heart and breathing through a stethoscope. Another doctor entered the room, and the two doctors talked to each other. Hector heard the one who was examining him say, "Improvement already," but he did not hear much else. The second doctor left, and the first one finished his examination.

"Mr. Gomez, this completes the medical procedure. The nurse will bring your clothes, and the guards will escort you to your cell. Tomorrow, you'll come back for tests like the kind you had on your first day here. After that, I, or another doctor, will be examining you every week for the next several weeks."

"When will I go before a judge and have my case heard?"

"I can't answer that, Mr. Gomez. It's for the local authorities to decide. I just deal with the medical condition of the prisoners."

Fifteen minutes later, he was back in his cell. Odd as the medical procedure had been, it had at least been something different. It didn't take long for the familiar tedium to set in.

When he went to the yard later that day, he found that three of the other prisoners had undergone the same procedure. All three had needle marks in both arms, and all three had been told they were necessary for more anesthesia. None of them had been told much about their conditions, and they did not know how long the procedure lasted.

Every day after that, a few more of the prisoners had needle marks and bruises on both arms. They were told the same things about their conditions and the procedure, and they all underwent a weekly series of physical tests and measurements.

One evening Hector paced back and forth across his cell. He paced a lot now, and did push-ups and sit-ups, to wear himself out so he would be able to sleep after the lights went out. When he was a child, he had been taken to a zoo. A tiger in its prime, big and strong, paced back and forth in his cage. He didn't belong there; he belonged in the jungle. Hector hated seeing that tiger. He ran away from the cage and the zoo and never returned. Now he was the tiger—caged-up energy he couldn't use but, more than anything, wanted to use. It wasn't a desire to get out and see his family and resume his old life. It was a desire to get out, be free, and do things—new things, different things, many things—that would challenge his body and mind. He wasn't even sure he could return to his old life if he were given the chance.

His mind was on fire as it never had been before. He was going to the library as often as he could, bringing back to his cell as many books as the prison permitted. Often he paced and read at the same time. Challenged—he hadn't felt challenged since he was much younger. Younger. Some of the prisoners had told him he looked younger, and he had said the same to them. At first he thought it was his mind playing tricks on him—prison did that to you—but it became more apparent with each passing day. And the other prisoners said they *felt* better, younger too, as Hector did. One of the oldest, Miguel, said he had his first erection in years. He smiled without answering when Santos, the compulsive asker of questions, asked, "What did you do about it?"

CHAPTER 8

THE FOUNTAIN OF YOUTH

In a top secret, secure, windowless, temperature- and humidity-controlled conference room, one of many such rooms spread randomly throughout a subterranean complex built to withstand nuclear warfare and its fallout, where the only computers were impenetrable Internet virgins that operated on the facility's private network and encrypted every keystroke typed on them, five men and women—whose attendance at the meeting was known only to them and the president of the United States—convened to discuss the results of an experiment so explosively controversial that it would be disavowed and terminated immediately if it were ever discovered or disclosed to anyone outside a small circle of high-ranking officials within the US government and the foreign government responsible for "hosting" the experiment. The position of the foreign government was so sensitive that the country was not referred to by name, only as "the host."

Dr. Anne Braxton, director of the National Health Administration, stood before a screen on which was displayed a chart, its columns filled with numbers. "The host initially obtained one thousand one hundred forty-nine test subjects. Demographically, ninety-four percent were in the prime grouping: eighteen to twenty-four years, the donors. The remaining six percent were fifty-five to seventy, the recipients."

"How were they 'obtained'?" Frank Harlow asked. He was the president's chief of staff and closest advisor.

"The host government conducted what was ostensibly a nationwide drug and terrorism raid," Zach Kruger, director of Centralized Intelligence, responded. "Extrajudicial disappearances are common there, and the locals know better than to ask questions. The test subjects were brought to a remote experimental facility funded by the United States, which was, in the interests of secrecy, built by several US Marine and Army Special Forces units under the ultimate supervision of General Mallice."

The group looked at the oft-decorated chairman of the Joint Chiefs of Staff, bedecked in his military regalia. He made no acknowledgement.

"I'm assuming the medical teams were American?"

"Of course, Frank," Braxton answered. She felt the annoyance common to career bureaucrats who had to answer to "temporaries" in the executive and legislative branch. "The age groups were separated, and the older group was extensively benchmarked. The procedure was performed on all sixty-nine of the older prisoners, although the project leader, Dr. Eckersley, felt that some of them were too old or were in too poor of a condition to benefit. The results—"

"Excuse me, Dr. Braxton," Harlow said. "Before you get into the results—and this may be repetitive for some of you here, but this is my first meeting—could you give me an overview of the procedure?"

"About eighteen months ago, researchers at the Jill Yates Foundation discovered a hormone-like substance they labeled prime hormone factor, or PHF. They determined that it was responsible for a dramatic extension of lab-mouse life-spans. PHF is only found in humans ages eighteen to twenty-four. The National Institute on Aging Research recognized PHF's potential and took control of the research. Even individuals eighteen to twenty-four have only trace amounts of PHF. However, NIAR biochemists developed a marker for it. Because of its instability and limited presence, donor blood has to be quickly drained and the PHF identified, then separated from most, but not all, of the blood. The PHF lasts longer if it is retained in some of the donor's blood. From that point, the procedure is essentially a blood transfusion, except the PHF and its blood are transfused from twelve to eighteen donors—whose blood is matched to the recipients—in rapid succession."

"Were either the donors or the recipients released after the procedure?"

Braxton stared at the chief of staff. Did he really not understand? "Removing all of the donors' blood ends their lives. As for the recipients, they are still at the facility so that we can continue measuring their medical metrics."

There was a long silence.

"So over a thousand people have disappeared or are dead as a result of this experiment. How does the host government explain that?"

"It doesn't," Kruger answered. "The host was chosen precisely because this sort of thing happens there and people keep quiet if they want to stay alive. Financial arrangements were made with officials within the government, a very small group restricted to those who had an absolute need to know. Paul has taken precautions to ensure there are no disclosures."

"In other words, all the right people have been bribed and blackmailed?"

"They've been incentivized and informed of compromising material," responded Paul Carson, the director of the Global Security Agency. He and Kruger, rivals for supremacy within the intelligence community, hated each other but shared a passion for euphemism.

"I'm sure these operations are absolutely necessary and in the best interests of the United States," General Mallice said sarcastically. "Let's just skip all that bullshit and get right to the point." His voice had the harsh quality of boots on gravel.

"Certainly." Dr. Braxton pointed at the chart on the screen with a laser pointer. The general wanted to skip the bullshit? She'd skip the bullshit. "We have found the fountain of youth. In the recipients, the average readings for every single medical metric—think of the multipage readouts you get from your annual physical checkup—every single medical metric shows substantial improvement. Not only is it substantial, but it has been ongoing; these prisoners are getting younger every day. I mentioned that Dr. Eckersley did not want to do the procedure on a few of the older, less healthy prisoners.

It was those prisoners who showed the greatest improvement, but there was not one prisoner who did not show statistically significant improvement across every metric."

Even Mallice looked astounded. "How many years have the prisoners regressed? I suppose that's not the right word, but you know what I mean."

"We've been using the term 'age reversed.' As of the end of last month, the estimated average age reversal was eleven point four years. The range was eight point four to sixteen point six years, but keep in mind the age-reversal process is still occurring; we don't know yet where it will settle out. It's not just age reversal either. We've seen malignant tumors vanish, chronic conditions disappear, even Alzheimer's stopped in its tracks and subsequent mental regeneration. It's been absolutely amazing."

"And all this is from a single application of the procedure?" Harlow asked.

"That's correct."

Carson whistled. "You could balance the budget with what geezer billionaires would pay for an extra ten or fifteen years."

Harlow nodded. "When the president authorized the experiment, I'm quite sure he didn't realize that it might have these kinds of ramifications. In its own way, this fountain-of-youth hormone may be as earth shattering as the atomic bomb. Imagine if this treatment were given to the right people. Imagine the leverage we could have if we could offer this treatment—to either friends or foes. I can't wait to tell the president about this."

"There's so much that could be done, and the public never need know about it," Kruger said.

"Aren't we getting a little ahead of ourselves?" Mallice asked. "You need twelve to eighteen prime-age donors for each recipient. Now maybe you can 'disappear' a thousand or so people in a Latin American banana republic and nobody makes trouble. You can only do that so many times in so many places. How are we supposed to get enough of these kids? Put up posters at recruiting offices: 'Come die for your country's leaders in a brand-new way'?"

Zach Kruger had made it to the top of Centralized Intelligence by never allowing moral considerations to enter into his calculations. "Obviously,

General, you are being facetious. However, what you say suggests a way around the problem with the prime-age cohort. To realize the kind of out-come we're envisioning, we will need a large number of people from that cohort, and they will all die. There is really only one acceptable way to kill large numbers of prime-age men and women."

"What's that?"

"I'm surprised, General, that you of all people would not see it immediately. We need a war."

CHAPTER 9

LEVERAGE

S peaker of the House of Representatives Stanley Portman sipped, and savored, his favorite bourbon. It came from a distillery in his home state of Kentucky. He had a long and mutually beneficial relationship with the distillery's owner. You couldn't go into just any liquor store and buy Tom Yarborough's bourbon. Tom maintained an artificial shortage that kept its price and cachet high. Not that Portman had to do anything so prosaic as buy his own liquor. His friend sent him several cases at Christmas every year.

It was a nice touch that the president had found a bottle and was serving it to Portman. You didn't get to be president by ignoring the nice touches, but this one made Portman apprehensive. In Decent America, you had a drink with a friend in fellowship to enjoy a simple pleasure together, loosen up, and trade jokes, observations, and confidences. In Damned America, alcohol was most often a weapon. It lowered defenses, elicited indiscretions, led to incriminating liaisons, and set up disclosures unpleasant and unethical, sometimes criminal.

But here he was in the heart of Damned America: President Lloyd L. Lochness's private sitting room, next to the Oval Office. The director of Centralized Intelligence, Zach Kruger, sat with Portman on one couch. The director of the Global Security Agency, Paul Carson, and General Arch Mallice, the biggest pain in the ass in the US military, sat across from them on another couch. Lochness, a big man who had played football in college, sat in his capacious black leather chair. Mallice was a teetotaler; the other men had bourbon.

When the leader of the free world (and the other political party) invited you for drinks late at night with the heads of the nation's two most powerful intelligence agencies and the chairman of the Joint Chiefs of Staff, you weren't there to discuss sports or other beanbag. Outside, a heavy rain beat on the windows, making the lights of Washington look like smeary blobs. On the way over in his limousine, Portman had wondered what this would be about. When he saw the other guests, he assumed the topic would be the ongoing war—or what Portman's party was calling the ongoing fiasco—in Syria.

"Stan," the president said, smiling. "What would you give to be twenty, twenty-five years younger? And I'm not just talking about feeling younger; I'm talking about being younger, actually reversing the aging process. You know, knocking the ladies dead in the sack and scraping 'em off the ceiling like we did way back when."

The last part was contradictory—dead women scraped no ceilings—but Lochness was not noted for the precision of his speech. It sometimes bordered on Berraesque, without Yogi's embedded wisdom. This was not, as Stan had imagined en route to the White House, a matter of the gravest national importance, announced in the most serious and somber of tones. "Uh, Mr. President, I guess we'd all like to be younger. But that's kind of an odd question, isn't it?"

"Not as odd as it might seem, Stan. It will seem even less so when I tell you what I'm going to tell you. We have a virtual fountain of youth within our grasp. This is a once-in-a-generation, maybe once-in-a-century, medical and scientific breakthrough. Researchers at the NIAR have actually figured out a way to reverse aging. They've confirmed it experimentally. The details, of course, are classified. Right now, at a secret facility there are some sixty men in their fifties, sixties, and even seventies who feel—and whose vital statistics indicate—that they're at least twenty years younger. They're in their...in their...thirties, forties, and fifties. The medical teams working on this project have said it's nothing short of miraculous."

So why, Portman wondered, were the spooks and the general here? There was more to this than some sort of tabloid-sounding miracle age-reduction formula. "I know I've been a critic of much government-funded research, but that's pretty exciting if it pans out." He sounded interested but not necessarily committed, an essential political skill.

"Exciting this definitely is, but some of the contingencies and requirements of the age-reversal process present some problems." Lochness pulled closer to Portman.

Here it comes—the catch, the yes-but. It had to be a doozy.

"The procedure uses what's called PHF, which stands for the hormone prime...uh, prime hormone factor. Now PHF is only found in people between the ages of eighteen and twenty-four, and only in very small amounts. It's my understanding that the PHF from anywhere from—I think it's twelve to eighteen younger people, is required to produce the age-reversal effect. The PHF has to be detected, quickly separated out, and given to the older recipient. Some of it is inevitably wasted. There is, however, an unfortunate side effect."

"What's that?"

"The donors die." Everyone looked at the speaker, General Mallice.

"The donors die?"

"Well, yes," Lochness answered. "Because they lose all their blood. They have to; it's the only way to get the PHF."

That was some side effect, one hell of a catch, the yes-but to end all yes-buts. Portman had a sinking feeling that this conversation was only going to get worse. Perhaps his best bet was to grasp the nettle. "So several hundred younger people died to reverse aging in the older people?"

"Over a thousand," the general said. You didn't get to his rank by being squeamish about death.

"What's happened to the older people?"

"They're still at the research facility," Lochness said.

"How long have they been there?"

"About fourteen months."

"Are they ever going to be released?"

"Eventually, when the researchers know the full extent of the age reversal. Anne Braxton told me that it's starting to slow down, and she thinks it will completely taper off within the next few months. When it does, the recipients will be released."

"But clinically they're at least twenty years younger?"

"That's correct. Braxton said the average is a little over twenty-two years. She thinks it will ultimately be about twenty-five. So let me repeat my question, Stan. What would you do to get twenty-five years of your life back? Because you can get them back."

You got to be Speaker of the House by listening to both what was said and what was unsaid. This was the offer, but God only knew what he'd have to do to accept it. Portman glanced at the spooks, then at Mallice. Somewhere in their computers, Kruger and Carson had a compilation of incriminating information on him, from his first traffic ticket to the swept-under-the-rug DWIs, questionable campaign contributions, and out-of-control parties, prostitutes, and affairs. And they were experts in fabrication, if need be. They—and Lochness and Mallice—had subordinates whom they could order to do anything they wanted done. This, then, was their leverage, the offer he couldn't refuse. So how would it feel to be thirty-nine again?

"How do we get the donors?" This simple question about a practical matter was meant as an indication that he was on board.

It was accepted as such. "In war, many young people die," Kruger said. "What we envision is a simulated war but with real casualties. Those casualties will be attributed to the war but will result from a large-scale administration of the age-reversal procedure. That operation will be conducted in the strictest secrecy. Syria, of course, offers the best opportunity for the war scenario, an escalation of the present situation."

"But we'll need other nations to go along with us," Portman said.

"Strictly speaking," Carson said, "we only need to get the leaders of nations, and perhaps a few trusted, operationally essential associates, to go along with us. We have a potent inducement: twenty-five years."

"How do you do an escalation that's not really an escalation?"

"General Mallice gets the credit on that one." Carson was kissing the general's ass. Everyone kissed the general's ass—not that it did them any good. The general threw sycophants under the bus just for the fun of it.

"We notch things up in Syria," Mallice said. "Way up—chemical and biological warfare. Of course, another nation or one of the terrorist groups will get the blame, but CBW allows two things. We can keep the media out on the grounds that it's too dangerous. Not that those blow-dried desk jockeys want to be near CBW or any other warfare. More important, we say that CBW requires inoculations for the soldiers. We can set up a facility in the middle of the supposed war zone that will allow for wide-scale execution of the age-reversal procedure."

And wide-scale execution of the soldiers. Portman bit his tongue, but his expression must have changed.

"Relax, Mr. Speaker. This is no more deadly or repugnant than a lot of other things we've done in the Middle East." Portman, an ardent Middle East interventionist, winced. Mallice glanced at Carson and Kruger. "Let's hope the secrecy on this one is better than it has been in the past."

"How many PHF recipients do you think there will be?" Portman asked.

"Best guess right now is around four to five hundred, but that could change," Lochness replied. "Obviously you've got to get the leaders in every country with an interest in Syria, and they've got their essential operational, intelligence, and military people. It will help with our media to offer PHF to key executives and controlling shareholders. Within the government—"

"I know five people who will be getting it," Kruger said. The other men laughed.

"Yes, and Paul, Zach, and Arch will have to determine how far down their respective hierarchies they need to go," Lochness said. "Stan, you won't be the only one in the legislative branch. We don't want to be too stingy with this. Refusal is not going to be allowed. Paul will handle any recalcitrants. Given the nature of what we're doing, the chance that anyone undergoing the procedure will later disclose it is virtually nonexistent."

"Are we absolutely sure about this procedure?" Portman asked.

"How can we be?" Mallice asked acidly. "We can't be absolutely sure until we have complete data on the recipients for the rest of their lives. Given that they've age-reversed twenty years or more, they might live another thirty or forty years. They've shown no negative side effects. If we don't do the age reversal, we'll probably go before they do, so waiting for full confirmation is not an option. NIAR researchers are now routinely replicating the initial experiment with lab mice that got this whole thing going. Some of the first mice have died, from the Jill Yates Foundation, but they were old—record-breaking old—for mice. Not one mouse in the experiments has shown negative side effects."

"Mr. President," Carson said, "we've heard from the Russians—"

"Paul, that needs to be discussed later."

"Certainly."

"Let's look at the actual operational details of what we're planning in Syria."

For the next fifteen minutes, they discussed simulating a major escalation of the Syrian war, until Lochness abruptly called the meeting to an end. He escorted Portman and General Mallice to the door, and the directors of Centralized Intelligence and the Global Security Agency remained.

"I guess there are going to be some details we're not privy to," Portman said to the general in the hallway outside the sitting room.

"Damn spooks run the country," Mallice said, shaking his head.

Back in the sitting room, the president refreshed everyone's drinks and sat in his chair. "You were saying about the Russians, Paul?"

"They've sent a long list of what they call 'safeguards.' They want all of our experimental data, and they want their own people doing the actual procedure. There's also a list of people they want as recipients."

"I said from the beginning that Raskolnikov would play ball. He's going to be the top dog until the day he dies. Another twenty-five years—no way he turns that down. Have they specified the people outside Russia among their allies they want?"

"No."

"What about the provocations?"

Carson and Kruger looked at each other.

"We're about eighty percent there," Kruger responded.

"And Maddox?" Dan Maddox was director of the Federal Investigations Bureau.

"About the same. We're meeting almost daily. We'll be ready, and the FIB will be too."

"Good." Lochness stood, and Kruger and Carson stood. "Gentlemen, to long life."

They clinked their snifters.

⋏

Russian Premier Rodion Roskolnikov and the head of State Security and Intelligence, Ivan Anokhin, sat across from each other in a small, windowless conference room deep within the Kremlin. It was one of the few rooms—accessible only with Roskolnikov's approval—where conversations could not be heard, where state secrets could be discussed and confidential orders given.

"So the Americans are, as they say, on the up-and-up?" Roskolnikov asked.

"They have met all our conditions and demands. Their protocols for lab mice have been verified, and so far our experiments with convicts have produced the same results as their experiment in Latin America."

"Technically, then, we could perform the procedures for Russian recipients in Russia. But with this phony escalation in Syria, there are supposed to be Russian casualties, so we might as well make good use of them and perform the procedure in Syria with everyone else. Just make sure that it is performed by Russians who have been thoroughly screened."

Anokhin nodded. Although he would be one of the recipients of the procedure, he was Roskolnikov's chosen successor and not overjoyed with the prospect of the premier's age reversal, which would allow him to rule Russia for that much longer. Anokhin chafed under Roskolnikov's megalomaniacal grip on power. The paranoid premier had a long history of replacing his number twos before they got their chance to become number one, a fate Anokhin worried ceaselessly he would share. Paranoia wasn't an occupational hazard in Russia; it was an occupational necessity.

"How far along are the Chinese?" Roskolnikov asked.

"Not as far as we are, but they have enough experimental confirmation; they are proceeding."

"Have we received the lists of recipients from Syria, Iraq, and Iran?"

"This week."

Roskolnikov put his head on the back of his chair and stared at the ceiling. "It was the American president Reagan who said, 'Trust, but verify.' Before we journey to Syria, I will place our military forces on full alert and move divisions to the Baltic and Black Sea regions and the western border. The Chinese will bolster their offensive forces directed at Taiwan, the South China Sea, and Southeast Asia. If there is any betrayal in Syria, even an accident or a blunder that adversely affects anyone important from Russia or its allies, within hours the United States will find itself in an authentic—not a simulated—multifront war it cannot win. Trust, but verify, and in the event of betrayal, strike."

CHAPTER 10

DELUGE

The Gulfstream G280 had just cleared the Cascades and the forest.

"Now comes the ugly part," Moustafa said to the jet's copilot, Ammar. Never talkative, Ammar nodded.

When people thought of the state of Washington, they envisioned its scenic western coastline, but the eastern half was as desolate as anything in Nevada, Utah, or Arizona. The midsize corporate jet, bearing east into the morning sun from Seattle, would be past the desolation in about twenty minutes, and it would take another few minutes to reach its destination, Coeur d'Alene, Idaho. Moustafa sipped his tea as the plane cruised at thirty-two thousand feet above the barren hills.

Home of Starbucks and Amazon, Seattle vied with San Francisco, Miami, and New York as the nation's trendiest and most desirable city. One of the four wealthy entrepreneurs on the jet, its owner, Tarik Aboul-Nour, had built Mt. St. Helens, his fashion imprint, from a T-shirt stand on a Seattle sidewalk to an online and international merchandising giant employing over twenty thousand people. Mt. St. Helens had made Puget Sound and the Cascades chic. Fashionistas in places where the temperature never dipped below seventy-five degrees sported its fleece-lined hoodies and burnished-suede hiking boots.

Aboul-Nour's father had brought his family to the United States in 1999, looking for the opportunity and freedom unavailable in Hosni Mubarak's corrupt and repressive Egypt. Seventeen-year-old Tarik completed high school and then one semester at the University of Washington before dropping out. Many of his Sunni coreligionists abhorred America; he embraced it, especially American business. He taught himself accounting from a used textbook purchased for a dollar. Sales he learned on the sidewalk. People liked his smile, his jokes, and his effervescence, buying far more T-shirts from him than his competitors. Soon he had a lease on a small store, which he jammed with an inventory that seemed to miraculously capture every trend just before it emerged.

From those beginnings he vertically integrated design, manufacturing, distribution, and retailing under the Mt. St. Helens's trademark: a white spiral above a green triangle. Building a brand around a deadly natural disaster may have been audacity bordering on foolishness, but it became part of the company's iconic allure. Within a decade the volcanic logo could be found in company-owned stores and high-end retail establishments in the United States, Europe, Asia, the Middle East, and Latin America.

Mt. St. Helens required its network of suppliers and contractors to pay the right wages, use the right materials, and follow the right environmental and labor policies. The right percentage of the company's profits was donated to the right causes. The company enjoyed mutually beneficial relationships with a number of tribes native to the Pacific Northwest, employing members and incorporating their symbols and designs—for which it paid royalties— into its clothing lines.

Wherever it located, the company hired from local Muslim communities. Its factories, distribution centers, and stores accommodated daily prayer services and observed Islamic as well as traditional American holidays. There was no pork in company cafeterias, no alcohol at company functions. Tarik had assimilated into American culture more than most Islamic immigrants, but his closest friends and most Mt. St. Helens's executives were, like Tarik, Muslims and immigrants from Egypt. So too were Moustafa and Ammar, the two on-call pilots of his Gulfstream. You trusted your pilots with your life, and required trust meant Egyptian Muslims.

Tarik had learned one lesson from American business: it paid to befriend politicians. He came from a baksheesh culture. The only difference in the American variety was the gratuities were larger.

Coeur d'Alene was the kind of junket the rich and powerful strove mightily to keep away from the media: three days of sybaritic schmoozing that gave influence peddling a bad name. A cabinet secretary and a Supreme Court justice, select senators, representatives (including the Speaker of the House), and bureaucrats, the governor of Idaho, and last, but certainly not least, the executives and lobbyists who were paying for it all would stroll the verdant fairways and manicured greens of the Coeur d'Alene Resort course (one green, reached by boat, floated on the lake), dine on gourmet fare, slurp expensive alcohol, and enjoy Las Vegas-caliber entertainment and prostitutes. It was billed as a conference so the sponsors would get a tax break. Guest speakers would make presentations on Important Topics, including Poverty and Powerlessness, and had to finish twenty minutes before the first tee times upon pain of not being invited to the next shindig if they didn't. Attendance at the presentations was strictly optional.

As the jet made its way across Washington to its lavish destination, Ammar noticed something odd. "Why are you turning north?"

"I'm not." Moustafa glanced at the flat-panel compass display. "But we're banking north." He rotated his steering wheel to correct, but it had no effect. The plane was heading almost due north. He rotated the other direction, but the compass registered no change in direction. The other instruments indicated that the jet was functioning normally. The altimeter showed no loss of altitude, and airspeed remained at Mach 0.80. He pressed the throttle. It stayed at Mach 0.80.

The jet was flying itself.

"What is happening here?" Ammar said.

"Something is wrong with manual override."

"But autopilot was not programmed to change course, and it cannot ignore manual commands."

"Remote operation?"

Ammar nodded. "This is a flying computer, and computers can be hacked."

"Someone has penetrated our systems."

A red graphic appeared on the center console display between the two pilots. "We just lost ground contact," Moustafa said. A blue graphic appeared. "And Wi-Fi and the phone. Whoever is hacking us just cut off our outside communication."

The cockpit door opened, and Aboul-Nour stood in the doorway. "We just lost the Internet," he said in Arabic.

"Yes, Wi-Fi is down," Moustafa said. "That's not the worst of it. Ground contact has been lost, and the jet is being remotely operated."

"Remotely operated? You mean you have no control of the plane?"

"Yes, that is what I mean. The plane has been hacked."

Tarik stepped into the cockpit, closing the door behind him. The cockpit had a two-way jump seat for a flight attendant, unnecessary on this short flight. Tarik sat in the jump seat, facing forward, obviously concerned.

The jet passed over the Columbia River and banked right. The compass display indicated it was now flying southeast, following the river.

"We're losing altitude," Moustafa said, pointing at the altimeter for Tarik.

"Does that mean we're going to land?" Tarik asked.

"It would have to be at Spokane. We are going in that direction, but our descent is too quick."

"And we are still at Mach point eight," Ammar said.

The cockpit went silent as the three men helplessly watched the plane lose altitude, almost as if it was going to land on the river below. There was a knock on the cockpit door.

"What's going on?" It was Donald Herd, a computer-networking billionaire.

"We're working on a problem," Tarik said. "It should be cleared up in a minute or two. I'll be right back there."

Herd said nothing and returned to his seat.

The plane continued to lose altitude, dropping below ten thousand feet. The three men's eyes stayed glued to the altimeter.

"We're getting close to Grand Coulee," Moustafa said. As if to confirm what he had just said, the massive dam appeared on the eastern horizon. The jet continued to descend.

Tarik voiced the awful suspicion. "We're headed toward the dam."

They sat in horrified silence. The jet was a thousand feet directly above the river and still descending. It was like a landing, but the landing gear was not activated, and the jet was flying at Mach 0.80. The cabin door flew open.

"What the—" Alfonso Redding, another billionaire, stared at the looming dam and the Grand Coulee Bridge just in front of it. "Holy shit!" he shouted. "Do something!"

There was nothing anybody could do. The plane was two hundred feet above the water and had leveled out.

"*Allahu akbar,*" Ammar whispered, and the other two Egyptians repeated it.

The jet cleared the bridge and slammed into the dam, penetrating the massive concrete structure a third of the way up its 550-foot height. There was a small explosion and a much larger one, opening a gaping breach. Thousands of cubic feet of water poured through, widening the breach. Blocks of concrete tumbled into the flow. The elevated road on top of the dam collapsed into the wall of water. Below the dam, the huge wave obliterated the Visitors Arrival Center, the Grand Coulee Bridge, and its eastern bank terminus, the town of Coulee Dam. Tiny Elmer City was hit next. Structures, cars, and people washed away like twigs and leaves on a stream. Sirens sounded and emergency alerts went out to the series of dams below Grand Coulee. They would be destroyed and the surrounding areas inundated as the flood wave made its way down the Columbia River Gorge. People had to be evacuated in the precious hours before it arrived.

⋏

Ted drained his second bottle of beer and watched the evening news. He hadn't watched the news much when Barbara lived with him; there were better things to do. He hadn't drunk as much beer, either. What an ugly breakup.

He could do no wrong when they met; he could do no right when they parted. Get over it; that was the way those things went.

The Grand Coulee Dam disaster was a made-for-TV bonanza; probably every household in America was watching. It was a wonder that there had been no crashes among the many local and national news helicopters flying over the churning mass of water rolling down the Columbia River Gorge. The ubiquitous eyes in the sky were matched by hordes of TV vans that had descended on the dams that would be washed away and the river towns that would be flooded by the surge in a projected twelve to twenty hours. Photojournalists stuck their microphones in the faces of people who were scrambling to load their possessions in their cars and trucks, facing the loss of everything—homes and businesses and, in a few heartbreaking cases, pets, stables, and horses—they had to leave behind. There were of course tears, but Ted was amazed at their politeness and even occasional gallows humor in the face of overwhelming adversity and overwhelming inanity. Maybe the TV vans wouldn't clear out in time. One could only hope.

The government and news media were already pronouncing Grand Coulee an open-and-shut case of terrorism. The two Egyptian immigrant pilots had shown no signs of radicalization, but neither had that couple in San Bernardino. The assumption gelled quickly that Aboul-Nour, a member of Seattle's elite with a place high on every list of progressive and humanitarian businesspeople, was probably an unwitting victim of his pilots. All the physical evidence at the collapsed dam had been blown up and washed away. The FIB and police had sealed off the pilots' houses, carried out boxes of potential evidence, and started questioning friends and family members.

Something had gestated within Ted for a long time, a vague feeling that had metamorphosed into a philosophical reorientation after the NIAR stole his team's Methuselah project. Like many scientists, he had never been particularly interested in politics. It was a weird, irrational realm inhabited by weird, irrational people. To spend time on it was to waste time much better spent on other pursuits. But politics was pushing to the point where it would not let him, or anyone else with a modicum of intelligence, ignore it.

An old friend and fellow scientist had remarked that there was now only three degrees of separation between the government and science. He was right. The tentacles were inescapably everywhere: universities, think tanks, foundations, research facilities, and ostensibly private enterprises. Even the few remaining inventors working out of their garages couldn't get far with their groundbreaking inventions before they ran into the government, one way or the other.

A reluctantly commenced examination of politics and government soon yielded skepticism, cynicism, deep suspicion, and revulsion, in that order. The whole system, Ted concluded, rested on mendacity, venality, stupidity, idiocy, incompetence, and corruption, a not-exhaustive list.

He got up from his couch and went to the refrigerator for another beer. So now the government and the media—and he had come to regard the latter as an arm of the former—were saying Egyptian terrorists steered a jet into Grand Coulee Dam. Within a day or two, if it was not already, the Internet would be full of skeptical questions, alternate scenarios, "suspicious" videos, purported new evidence, claims, counterclaims, and theories, all of them divergent from the party line. They'd chip away at the official story, and Ted had found that in so doing, the cranks, the mongrels, the tin-foil-hat-wearing conspiracy theorists, and the pajama-clad bloggers got it right more often than the blow-dried photojournalists, the official spokespeople, the pure-bred pundits and columnists, and all the other bought and paid for. Nobody was infallible, but on the Internet something happened that didn't happen in Official Story Land: people asked smart questions and tried to answer them.

Why, if you were going to go to the trouble of blowing up a dam, would you blow up Grand Coulee, with its relatively sparse population downstream, rather than say, Hoover Dam? Sure, Grand Coulee provided a lot of power, more than any other dam in the United States, but the terrorist focus to date had been on taking out people, not infrastructure. Besides, the electric grid had redundancies that would lessen the impact on power distribution. Taking out Hoover Dam would have killed a lot more people, and the loss of electricity would have wreaked havoc in high-population-density Southern California, not big-sky backwaters like Wyoming, Montana, and Utah. The corporate jet could have just as easily diverted south to Hoover Dam, which was well within its range.

The newsreaders said that the Egyptian pilots had worked for Aboul-Nour for five years, were considered trusted employees, and were highly paid. Why on earth would they give that all up for a suicide mission? Oh sure, sure, all Muslims were terrorists, but it was usually the poor and desperate ones who raised their hands, the ones with nothing to live for in this life but who would get their virgins in the next. Even more implausible was any notion that Aboul-Nour was behind it. Billionaires didn't take one for the team—any team, anytime, anywhere; life was just too sweet. Oh sure, sure, all Muslims were liars, but the pilots' and Aboul-Nour's wives and children were vehemently insisting that their husbands and fathers were nonviolent and had nothing to do with Islamic extremism.

Questions, questions, questions. Too bad all the evidence had been blown up or washed away.

CHAPTER 11

INOCULATION

The remaining inhabitants of Samquat, al-Magda, and Uglib, three small villages in central Syria, were awakened just after midnight. The light sleepers heard the distant whir that became a steady chop-chop. The roar of engines overhead woke the heavy sleepers. Helicopters were never good. Goats and sheep bleated. Children huddled on dirt floors, their mothers' arms around them. Marauding jihadist groups had seemingly come to a consensus definition of men—males who looked older than ten—and had conscripted them, leaving only younger boys and old and infirm men in the villages. A few of the boys peered out doors and windows—although they wished they were safely wrapped in their mothers' arms—because they were male and supposed to show their courage.

Something came from the sky, a mist the villagers felt but did not see in the darkness. The helicopters' whirlwinds blew it into their hovels, burning their eyes, noses, mouths, throats, and skin, making them cough. They clutched their chests, writhed on the ground, drooled uncontrollably, spat up blood, vomited, defecated, and urinated. And died. Within a quarter of an hour, everyone in the three villages was dead.

The world was not made aware of the tragedy for a week, and not without further tragedy. Outside of al-Magda, a dead sheep, blood matted on its face, failed to alarm two old women entering the village. Dead animals and people were common; they were buried and life went on. The women may not have understood the danger even as they smelled the stench and saw human corpses, perhaps concluding there had been a jihadist raid. By then it was too late; they had come in contact with the virulent agent and were soon dead. There were similar incidents in the three villages over the next few days, until someone took heed of the dead sheep, stayed out of al-Magda, and set in motion a chain of communications that finally reached officials at a UN refugee camp thirty miles away.

UN personnel in white hazmat suits uncovered the full horror: 315 people dead between the three villages. Nobody tallied the dead animals. The questions began as soon as the story hit the media. What kind of agent had killed the villagers? How had it been delivered? Why, and by whom?

Fortunately the US government was soon on the scene, providing answers—right or wrong—as only the US government could. It would take time to gather and transport samples of the deadly agent to a lab in the United States properly equipped to analyze them. Preliminary analysis suggested that the agent had been delivered from the air. It had to be helicopters, flying low and hovering over the villages, but no villagers were alive to confirm it. Which raised the question: from where had the helicopters come?

Helicopters were used by militaries, not jihadist groups. Syria was playing host to eleven, twelve, or thirteen—it was hard to keep track—foreign governments making war on its soil. Most of them, including the United States, quickly disavowed any connection between their helicopters and the attack. Then the US government let it slip that a "few" of its helicopters had been commandeered by shadowy terrorist groups over the past few months and that US intelligence also believed the same had happened to other countries' helicopters. So the United States narrowed the source of the suspect helicopters down to eleven, twelve, or thirteen governments and an unknown number of jihadist groups.

Not knowing what had been sprayed or who sprayed it did not stop US officials from speculating on why it had been sprayed. The three villages were predominantly Shiite. Inconveniently, the United States was backing Sunni groups, which it called rebels and everyone else called jihadists. The outside governments with which it was allied were also Sunni. The government couldn't let its Sunni allies take the blame, so US officials jumped to Full Convolution Mode. The villages, inhabited only by children, women, and sick old men, were nevertheless hotbeds of Shiite jihadism that had probably been wiped out not by Sunni jihadists but by rival Shiite jihadists. To their credit, most US newspapers that actually printed this "explanation" put it in the back pages, where few would read it. To their discredit, they did not question it, either in the stories or on their editorial pages.

⟁

Aubrey and her tent mate, Samantha, were awakened by Sergeant Griswold at 0300. "Fallout in thirty minutes," he said, and hurried to the next tent.

"What's going on?" Aubrey asked groggily.

"No idea," Samantha replied.

At 0330, 120 sleepy soldiers stood in formation, awaiting an explanation and expecting the worse. The Grand Coulee attack and the gruesome slaughter in the Syrian villages had transformed lukewarm American involvement into full-blown commitment: rebellion, regime change, and replacement with a US-friendly government. The three-R strategy would eradicate terrorism eventually, so the propaganda went, although it hadn't worked yet. It just needed more time, a generation or two.

Major Anderson addressed the company. "The recent attack on the three Syrian villages necessitates an expanded American presence here. The exact nature of the agent used in that attack is still unknown. As a precaution, troops in Syria will receive inoculations that offer the best protection possible against major known biological agents. In forty-five minutes you will board helicopter transports to an inoculation center. The trip will be about an hour. Do not eat or drink anything until after you have received your inoculations. Dismissed."

"I wonder why they don't bring the inoculations to the soldiers," Aubrey said to Samantha. "It's a lot easier to transport vials and needles than soldiers."

"Your guess is as good as mine. Maybe there's some benefit to centralizing everything and having it all done in one place. Wonder why we have to do this so freakin' early in the morning."

An hour later they climbed aboard a Chinook. Three transport helicopters ascended a few hundred feet above the landscape, invisible in the darkness. Aubrey checked her compass. They were flying southwest, toward the center of Syria. Everything about this little sojourn was weird. They were flying around 180 miles before dawn to get a shot. Weird, weird, weird.

Things got a little less weird when they reached their destination. The exact number of US military personnel in Syria was not disclosed to the public, but it was an estimated twenty to twenty-five thousand and growing. The helicopters landed not far from a structure of gray corrugated metal the size of an aircraft hangar. It looked large enough for the rapid inoculation of thousands of soldiers in a short time. Although transporting them burned a lot of helicopter fuel, doing it this way perhaps made more sense than tracking troops all over Syria.

Aubrey got off the helicopter and walked with the other soldiers toward double doors that opened as they approached. Inside, everything was as gray as it was outside. The cavernous facility was divided by a wall of gray corrugated metal and had a gray concrete floor.

There were ten desks set up in a line, each with a computer on it and a soldier sitting behind it. In back of the desks were mobile medical stations, with examination tables surrounded on three sides by curtains, stands with trays for medical tools, and various electronic instruments and monitors. Beyond the desks and medical stations were several rows of folding chairs. Apparently Aubrey's company would be the first to receive their inoculations; there was nobody ahead of them. While she waited in line, she sent a text to her mother. After a twenty-minute wait, a corporal behind a desk motioned for her to approach.

"Name and Social Security number?"

"Aubrey Elkington, six seven six, nine eight, four four one four."

The corporal typed the information into the computer. "Are you aware of any changes in your physical condition since your examination last month?"

"No."

"Private Elkington, proceed to that station." He pointed to one of the examination stations.

She walked to where she had been directed. A medical attendant carrying an iPad closed the curtain around the examination area and put on a pair of latex gloves. He glanced at the iPad. "Private Aubrey Elkington?" She nodded. "Private, we'll need a blood sample and a few measurements before we give you the inoculations," he said. "Please sit on the table." He took her temperature and blood pressure and checked her pulse and respiration. "Everything looks good. Any sicknesses or health complaints?"

She shook her head.

"Roll up your sleeve and clench your fist."

She did as instructed, and he tied a rubber strap around her arm. Her veins bulged. He rubbed her arm with cotton soaked in alcohol, stuck a needle in a vein, and collected her blood in two vials. After he put a square of gauze where he had drawn the blood and wrapped it with medical tape, he labeled the vials and left the examination station. He returned in a couple of minutes.

"Now you'll proceed to the seating area. We need to evaluate your blood sample before we administer the inoculations."

"Can I ask you a question?"

"Sure."

"Why do you need a blood sample for inoculations?"

"In a very small number of cases, recipients can have adverse reactions to two of the inoculations. There are blood markers that, if present, can indicate when a recipient will have such a reaction."

"I see. Thank you." She went to the seating area and sat next to Samantha.

"You know," Samantha said, "it would be nice if they had some orange juice or something, and maybe protein bars or cookies. I'm light headed, and we haven't had any breakfast."

"Major Anderson told us not to eat or drink anything until after the inoculations. I wonder why. You do that when you go in for an operation, but not for shots. This whole thing is really strange."

Samantha nodded. "Makes you wonder what they found in that stuff from those villages."

It was forty-five minutes before medical attendants began summoning soldiers, leading them through a door in the separating wall. Samantha was summoned, and five minutes later, an attendant came for Aubrey.

They went through the door in the separating wall. It opened into a hallway lined with rooms. The attendant checked his iPad. "You're in room fourteen." He led her to that room and opened the door. The room looked a lot like the medical stations, but Aubrey noticed that there was a gurney instead of an examination table. On top of the gurney was a clear plastic bag with a garment in it.

"Remove your clothes and put the gown on," the attendant said, pointing at the bag. "You can put your uniform in the bag."

"Why, if I'm only getting a shot?"

The attendant glanced at his iPod and smiled. The smile seemed artificial. "You've been in the army long enough to know better than to ask questions. I'm just following orders. Change your clothes, and you'll receive your inoculations in a few minutes." He left the room.

Slowly, reluctantly, Aubrey removed her uniform down to her bra and panties and put on the gown. In her seven months in Syria, Aubrey had been involved in attacks, had seen soldiers wounded and killed, and had been at risk of the same. She had never panicked, winning commendations for her performance under fire. Now, suddenly, she felt a niggle of panic, without fully understanding why.

The attendant reentered, carrying a tray with needles and syringes, followed by another man. From his lieutenant's insignia and the way he carried himself, Aubrey guessed he was a doctor in the medical corps. "Please lie down."

"For a shot…sir?"

The lieutenant looked at her coldly. "Private—" He didn't have to say more. The way he said "private" was the unmistakable and universally recognized tone with which officers dismissed the lower ranks. "This facility will process over two thousand soldiers today, so I'm quite pressed for time. I must administer your inoculations and be on my way."

She lay on the gurney.

The attendant swabbed a spot with cotton soaked in alcohol. The lieutenant took the plastic cover off the syringe and poked it into her arm.

Almost instantaneously Aubrey felt herself getting sleepy. A spasm of panic. This wasn't right, she wanted to shout, but an incoherent mumble was all she managed before she fell asleep.

CHAPTER 12

SERVICE

Next year, Connor vowed, he wouldn't come home for summer break. The only good thing about his job at the bowling alley was it made him want to stay in school and get a real job when he got out. There were a few old high school buddies to pal around with, but he missed his frat at IU. At least his father had decided he could pop brews at home, hang the drinking age. He sipped his beer and watched the evening news, which was filled with stories about Syria.

Aubrey was over there. Everything had gone all deep secret after the dam and the chemical and biological stuff. They still couldn't—or maybe wouldn't—say exactly what it was. He hoped she hadn't been exposed. Were all wars like this, where the people back home didn't really know what was going on? You could watch the news, but all they had to say was what the government told them, which wasn't much. Unknown chemical and biological agents were scary shit, so you couldn't really blame the government for wanting to keep out civilians and the media.

The pretty newscaster was gushing over that old windbag jackass Lochness. Who the hell cared that the president seemed more energetic, that this war had given him new purpose? Sure, he looked better on TV than Conner remembered, but politicians were like movie stars; they had makeup and lighting to make them look good.

The phone rang. Connor went into the kitchen to answer it.

"Hello."

"Connor?" It was Nora Elkington, Aubrey's mother.

"Yes."

"I have bad news." Her voice was shaky. She was crying, or trying hard not to. Something had happened to Aubrey. Not that, not that…please not that. "Aubrey's been killed in combat." She cried uncontrollably, and Conner started to cry.

"No, no," he whispered through his sobs. "This can't be."

"I'm so sorry. I know how you felt about her."

"This is so terrible for you…your family."

She cried a long time without saying anything. When it sounded as if she had stopped, he asked, "How did she die?"

"One of those big battles in the desert, where they might have used those gases. Al-Suk something or another. But she wasn't gassed. The army said it was mortar shrapnel. My baby…" She started crying again. "I need to be with my family. We'll let you know the arrangements."

He hung up the phone, sat on the couch, and cried. He had loved her, still did. Maybe there had been other guys for her, just like there had been other girls for him, but he loved her. Their first time together, two nights before she left, she laughed at the end. "I promised myself that my first time wasn't going to be in back of a car. Now you've made me go and break my promise." She ran her hands through his hair, they talked and laughed, and half an hour later they did it again.

His trip with her family to see her at the end of basic training had been bad. He was more sentimental, more emotional about separating from her than she was about leaving him. Maybe she was trying to be army tough. Maybe it was being surrounded by all those army guys. Or maybe she feared what might happen to her in Syria, and that was her way of saying good-bye. That could be it.

His father came into the living room. When Connor was twelve, he realized his quiet father knew many things that were left unsaid. He realized that if you were quiet, if you watched things and listened to people as his father did, you would be smarter than if you talked all the time. His father would know what had happened, because it was perhaps the only thing that could have made Conner cry. He sat down next to Conner, saying nothing, but resting a consoling arm on his son's shoulders.

⚔

Plainfield Presbyterian Church had been packed for Aubrey's funeral service. Connor cried throughout the service, not caring that his friends and most of his graduating class were there. The hardest part was the flag-draped casket. He thought of the lifeless body inside, what she had been, what she was no more. After the service, everyone was nice, caring, supportive. Classmates he barely knew hugged him. For that day, at least, the old high school rivalries and divisions were suspended.

Hundreds of people rode in the funeral procession, which snaked slowly to the cemetery northwest of town. Don Montrose drove the family. Connor wore the dark-blue suit he had worn on a date with Aubrey to Plainfield's nicest restaurant. After Mr. Montrose found a space in the already-crowded parking lot, the family walked to the bier above the grave. It hit Connor full force: Aubrey would soon be buried. He hung his head, and his mother put her arm around him. His twelve-year-old sister, Melissa, squeezed his hand. There were rows of white folding chairs facing the grave site, and the Montrose family sat in the second row. The day was cloudless and bright, ten degrees above comfortable, but not stifling like most Indiana summer days. The chairs filled, except for the front row, reserved for Aubrey's family. Some people had to stand.

"Military funerals are very powerful, very impressive," Conner's father said. Mr. Montrose had been in the navy and had seen his share. "There's an exact way that everything is done. The VFW pulled out all the stops. There aren't too many funerals anymore where there's a real-life bugler and not just a recording. They got a full casket detail and honor guard."

The honor guard—seven soldiers with rifles—and an officer stood in a line away from the audience. A bugler stood alone not far from the honor guard. Two rows of three soldiers, the casket detail, stood on the far side of an access road to the grave site. All the soldiers were in full-dress uniforms.

One member of the casket detail was an officer. On the other side of the road, another officer faced them. The two officers slowly saluted as the hearse drove up and stopped. The Elkingtons' blue SUV followed the hearse.

The hearse's driver stepped out, moved slowly to the rear of the vehicle, opened the rear door, partially withdrew the flag-draped casket, stepped away, and stood solemnly with his hand over his heart. In formation the casket detail marched forward, turned in unison toward the hearse, marched to it, and formed two lines facing one another. One of the soldiers advanced to the casket and pulled it out of the hearse. The others grasped the casket's rails and shuffled sideways in unison. They turned and slowly bore the casket to its bier. Once there, they stretched the flag above the casket, carefully centered it, and laid it back on the casket. Their movements were precise and coordinated.

Leonard and Nora Elkington got out of the SUV, then Danielle and Stacey, Aubrey's younger sisters. They walked arm in arm, supporting each other, to their seats in the front row and sat down. The Reverend Packard, who had performed the service at the church, stood beside the bier, holding a Bible.

"Aubrey Rosalind Elkington joins the long line of our members of the armed forces who have given their lives for our country. There are no words of praise or gratitude adequate to consecrate the bravery and the sacrifice of those who have fallen. Only God can do that, and we faithfully beseech him to do so..."

Connor couldn't concentrate on what the Reverend Packard was saying. His words at both the church and cemetery seemed more about Aubrey the soldier than about Aubrey the person. What he said about Aubrey the soldier could be said about most soldiers who died in combat: valor, sacrifice, service to God and country, blah, blah, blah. Why did she have to die? How did the death of a beautiful nineteen-year-old help anyone in the United States? Could the government even say for what cause she had died? Those questions weren't asked, so there were no answers. But those were the questions Connor asked. The military rigmarole, impressive and moving as it might be to some—it would be a comfort to her family—hid the possibility that her death was senseless and stupid. Wars were usually senseless and stupid.

"Lord, we ask that you take Aubrey—bright, vivacious Aubrey, so full of ambition and promise—we ask that you bless her and take her into your loving arms. She died far too soon, well before her time, but not yours. It is not given to us to understand your plan, but we understand that Aubrey's passage to you is part of that plan. Her family and many friends will never forget Aubrey, and we know in our faith that she has found peace in your shelter and love. Amen."

At least during the last part of the benediction the Reverend Packard hadn't said anything about war and Aubrey the soldier.

"Attention!" The honor guard officer commanded. The soldiers stood at attention. More military. "Stand by! Ready!" The soldiers simultaneously shifted their feet and assumed firing position. "Aim! Fire!" The shots were loud, jolting; Connor flinched. Fingers went into ears. The soldiers bolted their rifles. "Ready! Aim! Fire!" Another round of shots, and the soldiers again bolted their rifles. "Ready! Aim! Fire!" Another round of shots. The first notes of "Taps."

Connor couldn't help it—"Taps"—and started crying. Most everyone else did, too. Finishing the mournful call, the bugler saluted. With meticulous precision, the casket detail folded the flag from Aubrey's casket.

"There's a lot of symbolism wrapped up in that flag folding," Connor's father whispered.

The flag was folded a symbolic thirteen times into a neat triangle. Only its white stars and blue background were visible. The detail presented it to the officer. They stepped away from the casket. The officer walked to the Elkington family and knelt before Nora and Leonard, the flag in his outstretched arms. He handed it to Nora.

"Ma'am, this flag is presented on behalf of a grateful nation as an expression of appreciation for the honorable and faithful service rendered by your daughter." The officer stood, saluted, and stepped away. Nora and Leonard wept. He put his arms around her shoulders.

A cemetery official stepped to the front. "That concludes today's service."

People stood and walked back to their cars. The Elkington family remained seated for some time before they went to the casket. They knelt and placed their hands on it. Mother, father, and Aubrey's two sisters said good-bye. Nora stood, turned, and beckoned to Connor. He stepped up to the casket. She took his hands in hers.

"Spend a few moments with Aubrey."

The family stepped back, and Connor knelt before the casket. "Good-bye, Aubrey," he whispered. "I love you. I'll miss you…and I'll never forget you. Good-bye." He bowed his head, touched the casket, stood, and joined the family. Nora hugged him.

"Connor, I want to say this before the reception, when I might not have a chance. You're part of this family." Danielle and Stacey nodded. "I want you to come see us…often, whenever you want. Whether you feel like talking and visiting or just want to be in Aubrey's house and sit by yourself. It doesn't matter, but you come see us."

"Stop by the office when you get a chance," Leonard said. "Maybe you want to check out markets and finance as a career." He was a stockbroker. "Just call first and let me know you're coming."

Connor nodded. "Thank you."

⅄

The reception was at the community center. Connor found refuge with his old baseball teammates. There were several policemen and members of the city council in attendance, but nobody was checking IDs. The teammates, sitting at a couple of corner tables, had beers with their roast beef sandwiches and macaroni salad. Condolences were offered—"She was a great girl, we're going to miss her"; sorrow expressed—"I feel so bad for you, man"; support given—"Dude, let's hang next week." As the beer and fellowship flowed, Connor's despair and anger began to fade. He laughed at jokes and joined the discussion of college and professional sports.

There was always that one guy who didn't get that he was the joke. Morris Dunbar had just enough talent to land a spot on the baseball team, but not enough to get off the bench except when the team had a ten-run lead at the end of the eighth inning. He threw off the unmistakable aura of the chroni-cally insecure—"Like me, like me, like me"—which guaranteed that nobody would. If you were looking for a laugh on the team bus, you could always make a joke about Morris. Usually just as funny, often more so, were Morris's lame comebacks.

Morris approached the group, beer in hand. He probably didn't even like beer, just trying to be one of the guys.

"I'm sorry about Aubrey, Connor."

"Thanks, Morris."

"It must be quite a comfort for you, knowing she died for her country."

A perfectly wrong thing to say. Clueless Morris.

"Yeah, that makes her less dead," Connor said acidly. "She didn't die for her country; she died for her government so it can replace a gang of thugs and crooks in Syria with another gang of thugs and crooks."

Some of his teammates looked surprised. Morris, crushed, slunk away.

"I've had enough 'yay, yay USA' bullshit for today."

CHAPTER 13

DANGER

Ted was refilling his glass at the filtered water machine. He felt a tap on his shoulder and turned around.

It was Heather Lindholm. "Can you come to my office?"

"Sure."

They walked to her office. She motioned for Ted to sit in a chair she had moved behind her desk, next to hers. On her computer screen was a picture of President Lochness dated the previous year. She clicked again: another picture of Lochness, dated the previous week. She summoned a series of Lochness pictures, placing older ones next to current ones. Soon she had a montage.

She wrote on a pad and handed it to Ted. *Does Lochness look younger to you?*

He examined the pictures. Lochness did look younger in the more recent ones. He nodded and handed her the pad. She wrote on it and slid it back. *We need to talk.*

After work?

Yes. Ground Zero, at 6?

He nodded.

They met at the appointed hour at Ground Zero, a bar and restaurant with curtained booths, quiet and private. He was surprised she ordered chardonnay. She didn't drink at company functions, and he had assumed she didn't drink at all. He ordered a scotch and water. The waiter returned in a couple of minutes with their drinks, two menus, and a wine list. Ted said nothing about the menus. Having a drink with his forbidding boss was a milestone; dinner might be a bridge too far.

"Lochness's wasn't the only portfolio I compiled," she said, pulling a sheet of paper from her purse. "Recent pictures of many of the high and mighty are getting harder to come by, even on the Internet. But I got the vice president, Directors Kruger and Carson, Secretaries Longmire, Tolan, Parkhurst, and Kormatsu, Generals Mallice and Bradford, Admirals Greene and Hornburg, Chief Justice Mortenson, Speaker of the House Portman, Senate majority leader Hernandez, and chair of the Federal Reserve Collins, among others. That's just the top tier in government, there are others. Business and media people you'll recognize, including our own Jill Yates." She handed him a DVD. "You can see for yourself. Obviously I couldn't send this e-mail."

"They've all found the fountain of youth?"

"Every one of them, apparently."

"It's got to be PHF."

"Has to be. They've turned your research into an antiaging elixir for the elite."

"Elite elixir—catchy. Maybe we could trademark it."

She smiled. He could count on one hand—okay, maybe two—the number of times he'd seen her smile. Did it change things in some subtle way? Was it the smile of an ally? Proceed with caution.

"So many questions," he said. Had the NIAR discovered how to extract enough PHF from a human or humans to transfuse it and reverse aging in the recipient? Had PHF been analyzed and synthesized? How had they kept it stable? Where had the eighteen- to twenty-four-year-olds come from?

"What bothers me the most is the secrecy," she said. "They took the project from us and told us to be silent about it. We never heard another word, but suddenly all these powerful people look like they went to some Beverly Hills plastic surgery clinic—"

Ted laughed. "Lochness looks better, more natural, than he ever would with plastic surgery."

"Most of them do."

The waiter appeared. "Can I refresh your drinks?"

"Let's order dinner," Heather said, glancing at the menu. She didn't wait for his nod. "I'll have the grilled salmon with asparagus and roasted potatoes. And more of this chardonnay."

"The rib eye, medium rare, with the garlic mashed potatoes and wedge salad. And a Dos Equis, draft." He felt a pleasant anticipation. Having dinner with the Ice Queen might give him a peek under the Nordic reserve, especially if she kept drinking. That wasn't all he'd like to peek under. Don't even think about it, Ted. Although, truth be told, her deliberately utilitarian wardrobe didn't hide the well-proportioned figure and the long, shapely legs. And there was nothing unpleasant about the wide-set blue eyes, blond hair swept to one side, desirable lips, and the alert, intelligent cast to her reasonably attractive face. She was in her early forties, about Ted's age. Beautiful? Not really, but looks grew on you if you liked the person. Hers were growing on him. Wonder what she was like in the sack. Forget it, forget it, forget it. Nobody with a three-digit IQ played around with the boss.

They tossed back and forth various conjectures about what the NIAR and the government had done with PHF until their dinner arrived. He didn't know whether Ground Zero was part of a chain, but if it was, the food was surprisingly good.

"Do you have a family, Ted?"

They'd been working together for over three years, and she didn't know whether he was married. He knew she wasn't, but he didn't know much else. "No, I'm not married."

"Girlfriend?"

Was she supposed to ask that kind of question, being a boss and all? He wouldn't sue. "I had one. We broke up a few months ago. You?"

She had a faraway look, perhaps recalling some Nordic Adonis from her past. She shook her head. "No, nobody. I overwhelm men with my vivacious personality."

Wow! Self-aware sarcasm—a first. "That must be it."

"Why don't men like intelligent women?"

What the hell was he supposed to do with that? It had been a long day. He was tired—plus he'd had a couple of drinks—too tired to be clever. Too tired for anything but candor. "Can I tell you something about men?"

"Please do. I find them hard to understand."

"That's because you're trying too hard. Men may be nature's simplest creatures. When a normal, straight male meets a female, within a minute he's checked her out and formed a first estimate on what she'd be like in bed and his prospects for getting her there."

She looked interested, but interested as if he were describing a new lab procedure.

"If she checks out and he goes for it, then sex becomes the prime directive. Her brain can be a huge obstacle, especially if the guy is full of shit. Most guys are, at least when it comes to women."

"It can't be that simple."

"Well, here I am, trying not to be full of shit, and you don't believe me. Most women want the BS." He hoped the "most" excepted present company.

"So you're saying that I'm your boss, we're in a working relationship, but when we first met, within a minute you were thinking about sex?"

"Yup."

"But you haven't 'gone for it,' as you say."

"Of course not. I'm not an idiot, and you're my boss."

"And what if I weren't your boss?"

Danger! Danger! Danger! "Then I might go for it." Oh you fool!

"I have my résumé out, and I've interviewed at several places. I'm pretty close to an offer from another company."

"You're not joking?"

"How often do I joke, Ted?"

Wow! He said nothing, letting it sink in. What a strange evening. She might be leaving Jill Yates, and that wasn't good. She wasn't a warm and fuzzy boss, but he respected her and liked working for her. But then there was this thing that might be developing between them. That had a far better chance if she wasn't his boss.

"I've got mixed emotions about you going somewhere else. On the plus side, I'd be more inclined to go for it…right after your farewell party."

She leaned toward him, looking directly into his eyes. "Why wait?"

Within forty-five minutes they were at her apartment. He opened a bottle of wine and poured a couple of glasses. She went to the desk in her living room, which featured a panoramic view of Mission Bay. He had brought the DVD she had given him earlier. She slipped it into the computer on her desk.

"Just look at these pictures." He handed her a glass of wine and watched as she clicked through the DVD. Seeing the various men and women whose photos she had compiled had a cumulative impact. They all looked indisputably younger.

"They've figured out how to use PHF, and they've cooked up some sort of perpetuity project," he said.

"And what are the chances that the rest of us will see the benefits of this perpetuity project?"

"Remote to nonexistent would be my guess. Death is the only thing that stops these bastards, and now they've figured out a way to cheat it. Why would they give that to the masses?"

"How come nobody is talking about this, in the newspapers or TV?"

"You have to see it in a compilation, like you've done, before it really hits you. As for the media, they're bought and paid for. If they're told to ignore something, they'll ignore it. Since we lost our mice to NIAR, I've been on the Internet a lot. It's not perfect—there's boatloads of crap—but you find out things you never find out if you stick to the mainstream. Let me show you something."

She stood. He slipped into her chair and typed a web address to a YouTube video. "We've been told there were no videos of that plane crashing into the dam. Watch this. I can't vouch for its authenticity—nobody can—but it's gone viral."

From a vantage point to the right and above the dam, on some sort of hill or bluff, the video picked up the jet just before it cleared the bridge in front of the dam. Whoever shot it was understandably shaky, but the quality was fairly good. The jet hit the dam, and there was an explosive flash. Then, a second or two later, there was another, much larger flash from a spot some distance from the first flash. The dam crumbled, and a wall of water powered through. At that point the video ended, as whoever shot it presumably raced to higher ground.

"That second flash," she said. "How did it happen? Where did it come from?"

"There are all sorts of theories on the Internet. It's like the Zapruder film and the Kennedy assassination. The video matches up with some still photos of Grand Coulee, but who knows what somebody might have put together with today's technology. What if it's real, though? Did the second explosion come from the plane? Why was it so much bigger, and why was there that time and distance between the two explosions? If the second explosion didn't come from the plane, that gets into some truly awful possibilities. If it came from the dam, it would have to have been preset. Only the government would have that kind of access."

She put her hand on his shoulder. "Run that video again."

They watched the video three more times. She left her hand on his shoulder, and her leg brushed against his. She reached over him, her breasts tantalizingly close to his face, and clicked off the computer. "Let's sit on the couch."

He detoured to the kitchen for the bottle of wine, refreshed their glasses, set the bottle on an end table, and set himself close to her on the couch. The discussion of PHF and Grand Coulee Dam, momentous as the implications may have been, didn't last long. She subtly shifted her position; she was right next to him. The invitation was clear. He kissed her lightly, then more passionately. She responded, unmistakably. The Ice Queen was melting! He moved down her neck while groping for the top button of her blouse. She took his hand and stood. He knew where they were going.

She stopped in front of her queen-size bed and turned to him as she unbuttoned her blouse. "I like it slow, and I like it relaxed." She smiled impishly. "At least at the start. Nobody takes time to enjoy things anymore."

Her idea of "enjoy": the most tantalizingly torturous, mind-blowing, inside-out, upside-down sex Ted had ever had. Stroking, probing, rubbing, tickling, nibbling, biting, licking, and kissing, she turned his erogenous zones, some of which he was unaware, into raging hot spots of arousal. She took him to the brink of unbearable pleasure, relented, then to another brink, in a way that could, oddly enough, be described as methodical and precise, but left him begging for release. Those Scandinavians. And she treated his body and its appendages as instruments for her pleasure. He reciprocated in a way that he never had with a woman. Letting her guide him, he took her to the brink, relenting, resuming, relenting, learning more about what gave a woman— this woman—pleasure than he had in all his previous sexual encounters.

The barely bearable reached unbearable, and then a gasping, moaning, shattering summit and ecstatic release. He was panting harder than he had after last year's half marathon. They were spent. He rolled onto the bed. She nestled next to him, and he put his arm around her. They said nothing for a time. Nothing needed to be said.

She was the first to stir, rolling to the side of the bed and standing. "I need to step away," she said to the exhausted, insensate blob formerly known as Ted. "Can I get you a beer?"

Half-asleep, he murmured, "That would be great."

"Can we share it?"

"Share and share alike."

She brought a cold beer. It sparked a rally. The second time was just as good, if not better.

CHAPTER 14

SLEUTHS

P eter Valencia called himself a "technuman," to his father's dismay. If he had had friends other than the kind made online, they would not have been surprised or dismayed, but he had no such friends. When he was probed by flesh-and-blood humans searching for polite ways to ask, "What the hell is wrong with you?" they received an unemotional stare that left them feeling like inanimate objects. Peter acknowledged no syndrome or place on a spectrum. Rather, he responded, he was the next evolutionary step, a hybrid between technology and human. Then he went back to ignoring them.

By credit hours, the fourteen-year-old was a sophomore at the University of Texas at Austin. He was enrolled in two graduate-level computer science courses. But for the child labor laws, he could have had a full-time job with any of Austin's computer companies. They would just have to wait, but they already knew about him.

Carlos Valencia got up at six thirty and made his way to the kitchen for the essential first cup of coffee. On the way to his office, he stopped by his son's room. The door was open, and Peter was on his computer. The probability was evenly split between whether he had been up all night or had caught a couple of hours sleep. He fell asleep when he got tired, and two hours was usually restorative.

Peter looked up from his computer. "You'll find this interesting."

Carlos entered the room. If his son said something was interesting—and it was comprehensible to non-technumans—it would be interesting. "What do you got?"

"Check out this video of supposedly recent combat in Syria."

"Supposedly?"

Peter clicked on the video, war footage in which a US-backed Syrian rebel unit overran what was identified as a Syrian terrorist unit, capturing and displaying a black banner with white Arabic writing. Americans and Syrians shook hands, shouted, and triumphantly hoisted their rifles in the air. The video ran for about two minutes.

"Here's another video." A caption said *Iraq 15/04/2004*, but it was the same video. Peter pulled up several other videos purportedly of Syrian combat with matching videos dated from 2004.

"How did you discover this? Somebody has it on the Internet?"

"No, I found the dated videos on my own. I hacked a Department of Defense information agency."

Carlos shook his head. He had warned his son repeatedly that his hacking would get him in trouble. Peter, confident of his ability to elude detection, went right on hacking. A curious trait of autistics: they rarely lied. Carlos no longer knocked on Peter's bedroom door when it was closed. The last time he had done so, Peter had calmly told him he was masturbating and asked him to come back later. He was no less forthright about hacking. Carlos hadn't really been astonished by the masturbatory admission and was rather relieved that his seemingly asexual son was so engaged. He was curious about the images he may have had on his screen. Human or machine?

"Illogical." That was one of Peter's favorite adjectives.

"What?"

"If the military is going to rely on old videos to convince the public a war is occurring in Syria, it should have a much higher level of security for the old videos. Unless these videos were meant to be discovered."

When it came to the government, Carlos had found that "stupid" was a correct assessment more often than "diabolical," but the videos posed a conundrum. If the military had stupidly failed to secure the old videos, then it might be "fighting" a fake war. It probably had some sort of diabolical purpose for doing so. If, on the other hand, the old videos were meant to be discovered, that too might indicate a diabolical purpose, but what that might be was a mystery.

There was, perhaps, a way to get more information.

"Can you get these videos up on the Internet, side by side, without anyone knowing where they came from?"

"Yes."

"Okay, don't do it now, but I may want you to in the next few days. I'll tell you when."

⅄

Leonard Elkington emerged from his office at Paramount Securities and approached Connor in the reception area. "So glad you decided to come by, Connor," he said. They shook hands. "The market ran up on that Fed announcement, and I got a lot of calls. Things are quieting down now, so we should be able to talk."

They went to Leonard's large office. There were numerous plaques on the wall and replica tombstones—financial publications' advertisements of initial public offerings—in Lucite on the desk and bookshelves, befitting his status as a big producer. Connor sat in a chair in front of his desk.

"I'm glad you've been stopping by the house. Nora and I aren't 'we must do lunch someday' type of folks. She meant it when she extended the invitation at the funeral, and she really likes it when you come by. So do you think you might have an interest in finance?"

"I took a class last year. It was interesting. Had a good prof. I enjoyed it." Connor noticed that Elkington's eyes never strayed far from the computer screens on his desk.

"I've been thinking, how would you like working with me the rest of the summer as an intern? You could reorganize my files on the computer, and I'm sure I can find enough other things to keep you busy. It would be a real-world education in markets, and you'd be getting paid."

Connor smiled. "I don't know. I was considering an exciting career in bowling alley management."

Leonard laughed. "I wouldn't want to take you away from that."

"Mr. Ruggerio was being nice when he gave me the job. He won't mind letting me go. When do you want me to start?"

"Next Monday."

"Thanks, that's quite an opportunity."

Leonard glanced at a computer screen. "Darn it."

"What?"

"Military Weapons Systems is down another half. You would think, with a big war going on, that the defense contractors would be the place to be. But they've been flat to down since that damn dam break, and I put a lot of my clients in them. Usually, even a hint of war and the defense stocks run up."

"Speaking of the war, Mr. Elking—"

"If you're going to start working here, let's drop 'Mr. Elkington' for 'Leonard.'"

"Okay, Leonard. Mrs. Elkington—"

"And go with 'Nora.'"

"That text Nora showed me the other day, the one before Aubrey got inoculated. She said it was the last one she received. She said they texted quite a bit, but that text was sent a week before Aubrey was killed. Doesn't that seem a little strange? No texts for a whole week?"

"Well, they went to a combat zone. Aubrey's unit was probably up to its eyeballs in alligators. Or they may have been prohibited from using their phones. We didn't get texts when she was in other combat situations, so that didn't bother me. But I'll tell you what's strange."

"What?"

"Nora's been trying to find people who lost loved ones in Syria. She's a big believer in, you know, support groups. She contacted the army, but all she got was the runaround. It seems nobody has a list of people who were killed in Syria. No names, much less addresses or other contact information. Nothing. She went on the Internet. Nothing there, either. All she could find were online obituaries. If I didn't know better, I'd say the army's trying to keep a secret."

⋏

Carlos Valencia scrolled down the long thread of comments elicited by the most recent article on his blog, NoneoftheAbove.com. Peter had posted the videos he had hacked from the Defense Department side by side with the purportedly recent videos of Syrian conflict. He had assured his father that all Department of Defense computer gumshoes would find was a server in a remote corner of Malaysia. Carlos reposted the pictures in his article, which questioned whether the American people were getting the true story about Syria.

There were the expected comments. Plaudits from the gang who liked everything he wrote. Hatred and poison from those who didn't: *conspiracy theorist, anti-American asshole, idiot, jerk, douche bag, faggot, get a real job.* Progovernment propaganda, wooden prose so stridently over the top it obviously came from paid trolls. Odd subthreads that diverted into entirely different subjects: last summer's trip to Nova Scotia, the virtues of protein diets, cats, UFOs. Spam links to sites that would improve one's health, erections, or finances. Those he deleted. The ones that got his attention were from members of the military and from friends and relatives of those who had died in Syria. He noticed one in particular. It came from a Leonard Elkington, which sounded like a real name rather than a cute Internet moniker.

> *I don't normally comment on Internet sites. However, my daughter was in the army and died in Syria. There are some things that don't sit right with me. Other commenters have said that Mr. Valencia has disrespected those who have died in Syria. I understand how people feel, but I think he may be onto something. One thing I have found out since Aubrey's death is that the army will not release a list of those who died or were wounded in the central Syrian battle zone. Searching the Internet, I have been unable to find such a list, although over two thousand American men and women in the military were killed. In my Internet searches,*

I have also been unable to find the name of a single soldier who was wounded in central Syria. That seems odd, because the wounded usually outnumber the dead in war situations.

I encourage Mr. Valencia to keep digging. Maybe the truth is quite innocent, but the videos featured in this article suggest otherwise. If any reader knows of anyone who was wounded in these recent battles in central Syria, or has any other information, please post it.

Mr. Elkington's comment had elicited a lengthy subthread. Several posts from family members of dead soldiers confirmed similar experiences and frustrations trying to obtain the names of those killed. There was a comment claiming that Jasper Hewitt of Maplesville, Alabama, had been wounded in central Syria. The poster's name, ProudAmerican, looked familiar, and Carlos scrolled back through the comments. Just as he thought, ProudAmerican had an earlier post—wooden prose and that over-the-top government propaganda. ProudAmerican was a troll.

Yes, Mr. Valencia was going to "keep digging." He would check out this Jasper Hewitt in Alabama. If that story didn't wash—and he didn't think it would—he'd start calling every veterans hospital in the country, looking for soldiers wounded in Syria. It would be tedious. Too bad there wasn't an easier way.

Maybe there was. Carlos stood, stretched, and went down the hall to Peter's room. Fortunately, the door was open. Peter was at his desk, on the computer.

"I need another hack. After the last one, this one may be more difficult. The government has probably increased its security."

"What do you need?"

"A list of all the soldiers killed in central Syria. If possible, I'd also like a list of those who were wounded."

Peter nodded. "I'll get to work on it." He started typing.

"Listen, if it looks like the security is too tight, if there's any possibility the government could find out you're doing this, stop. For some reason, this may be very sensitive information. They haven't released it to people who have good reasons for asking for it. So be very careful and back away at the first sign of trouble. This isn't worth going to jail over."

Peter continued typing.

CHAPTER 15

ANOMALY

The prisoners all had chores—working in the kitchen, cleaning the communal shower, hosing down cells. Hector and another man, Rico, swept the yard twice a week, when none of the other prisoners were there. Although it was mundane and mindless, Hector regarded it as a good job. It was usually not hard work, he was outside, and he could talk with Rico. Today, however, it was a struggle.

"What's wrong with you?" Rico asked. "You're barely pushing your broom. Are you trying to make me do all the work?" He smiled.

Hector shook his head. "I'm not feeling well. You don't have to do the whole yard, but I have to sit down for a few minutes." Without waiting for Rico's response, Hector walked to a corner and slumped against the wall.

He felt hot and flushed. Although it was a cool day by tropical standards, he was sweating. His stomach didn't feel right either; he had to puke. He tried to stifle it, but that didn't help. It never did. The unwanted sensation rose up through his stomach and throat. He leaned over, expelling a noxious orange stream on the wall and ground.

Rico heard the sound, looked at Hector, went to the door, and knocked. A guard opened it. Rico pointed toward Hector. "He needs a doctor." The guard went back inside.

Within a few minutes, three medical attendants arrived with a stretcher. Feeling weak, Hector did not stand but rolled himself across the ground and onto the stretcher. Two of the attendants carried him while the third tried to ask him questions.

"How long have you felt sick?"

"Since this morning," Hector whispered.

"Have you been throwing up all day?"

Hector shook his head and held up his index finger: this was the first time. They left the yard, and he was carried through the cell block. The bright lights overhead made him feel worse. He hung his head to the side of the stretcher and vomited again. He would vomit twice more by the time he reached the medical facility. When he got there, he was no longer overheated but chilled and shivering. He was transferred to a hospital bed and covered with blankets. Several nurses and doctors came to his room. A nurse took his temperature and blood pressure, and two others hooked him up to various monitors.

"One hundred three and a half," one of the doctors said. He was an American. "Repeated vomiting. This is the tropics; he could have picked up any number of things."

"Perhaps it's related to the procedure," one of the other doctors said. She was an American, too.

The first doctor glanced at Hector and shook his head. "Tropical diseases afflict people of all ages. The patient's immune system should be exceptionally well equipped to deal with whatever this is, especially for a patient his age."

Hector motioned to a nurse and rolled on his side. The nurse brought a plastic bowl. Hector dry-heaved several times, producing only a trickle of thin yellow bile. The nurse wiped his mouth with a wet cloth and left the bowl next to him on the bed. His throat, mouth, and nostrils were burning from the vomit. The muscles in his leg and back were starting to ache. The doctors talked among themselves and issued what must have been orders to the nurses, by the way they scurried around. It was growing increasingly difficult to understand what anyone was saying. His ears were ringing. He made out one of the doctors saying, "Try to stabilize his condition."

Twelve hours later, Hector awoke from a feverish semiconsciousness and dimly realized he was very sick, much sicker than he had ever been. He tried to stir but could barely move. A nurse wrote on her clipboard and then put a cool wet cloth on his forehead.

"Mr. Gomez, can you hear me?"

Hector nodded weakly.

"Do you understand what I'm saying?"

He nodded again.

"The doctors are trying to determine why you're sick…"

Hector could not listen. He had a horrible pain below his stomach, clenching his asshole against what he knew was coming. It did no good. A foul-smelling deluge burst forth, spreading beneath him on the bed. The nurse pressed a button on the wall and started talking. He heard snatches of what she said.

"Massive rectal bleeding…extremely elevated temperature…oxygen… ER."

He was convulsing and drooling uncontrollably. The nurse put a mask over his mouth and nose. The pain wracking his body so overwhelmed him that his only thought was that he could not think. He felt a needle go into his arm, his last waking sensation.

Four days later, Hector's brain had stopped functioning; he was vegetative. Five days after that, Dr. Aldous Eckersley, head of the medical facility, authorized the withdrawal of life support and ordered an autopsy.

ᴧ

Dr. Anne Braxton glanced at her phone. An *EXTREMELY URGENT* caught her eye. Dr. Phillip McKinney, her number two at the National Health Administration, had texted her.

Must speak with you immediately. EXTREMELY URGENT. Highest sensitivity. I am in the first conference room on the right outside the auditorium

Be there soon, she texted back. However, she was the next scheduled speaker at a conference: Public Health Menace: The Scourge of Sugary Sodas. She beckoned to the conference moderator, Dr. Cynthia Charnow.

"Something has come up that I have to attend to. Can you rearrange the schedule of speakers so I can present later?"

Charnow nodded. "Dr. Culpepper and Dr. Zerwas are both here. If they went first, it would give you at least half an hour."

"Thanks." Braxton rose from her seat, walked out of the auditorium, found the conference room, and opened the door. McKinney was seated at the far end of a rectangular table.

"What's up?"

"Close the door," he said. She took a seat next to him. "One of the prisoners in our study died."

Braxton went white. "How?"

"Quickly and horribly. The prisoner's systems and organs shut down in a very short period of time. From the first symptoms of vomiting and high fever to brain death was about four days, although Eckersley kept him alive for another five."

"Could it have been shigellosis, or some other tropical disease?"

"This was much more virulent than most such diseases. The autopsy found nothing."

"So there's been an autopsy already?"

"Of course."

"Are there any indications that the death was due to the age-reversal procedure?"

That was the big question, and not just as a professional matter. Both McKinney and Braxton had received the transfusion treatment in Syria. "No. However, there are no indications that it wasn't. The nature of the patient's death rules out a lot of potential alternatives."

There was a long silence as they both tried to come to grips with various possibilities, including the possibility that they might eventually be afflicted with the same fatal malady that had killed the prisoner.

"Anne, I'd be lying if I said that I wasn't concerned about my own situation. But setting that aside, we've got to make a decision what to do about this. I think we need to let President Lochness know what's happened."

Braxton leaned her head back against her chair and gazed up at the ceiling. "In other words, let him know that our agency may have initiated the biggest medical fiasco ever, which could lead to the deaths of the most important people on the planet, including the president himself? Now let's just try to think about this. This death is probably due to something completely unrelated to the procedure, perhaps an especially deadly strain of some indigenous disease. If we go to the president and that's the case, it will look like we panicked, and we'll be idiots. That would probably be a career decision."

"My career isn't exactly my first concern here. If we tell the president now, we know that regardless of bureaucratic fallout, he'll move heaven and earth to try to determine what's happened, and to find a solution if the procedure killed the prisoner. If a cure is to be found, better sooner than later, if you know what I mean."

"I appreciate what you're saying, Phil, but until we know more, I want to treat this death as an anomaly. I see no reason to get everyone stirred up, when I think the chances that this is related to the procedure are fairly low."

"No reason to get everyone stirred up? I'm not talking about throwing hand grenades for the sake of throwing hand grenades. I'm talking about getting people mobilized to find out what went wrong and fix it. How can a prisoner who's had his age and immune system reset backward twenty-five years be so susceptible to whatever this is? From perfectly healthy, supposedly enhanced healthy, to dead in four days, out of the blue?"

"We're not going to raise any alarms until we have more information. That's my decision."

⅄

A week later, Braxton received a text from McKinney.

Second third prisoners sick same symptoms as first

It felt like a hard punch to the stomach. She thought she might be physically ill. Her hands shook as she typed out a reply.

> *Need damage control plans for all contingencies. Meet my office 4. Will notify appropriate people of developments, including pres. Immediate mobilization of NIAR researchers and resources.*

CHAPTER 16

MENGELES

The phone was ringing. Heather reluctantly awoke and fumbled on her nightstand for it. The display read *3:34*. "Hello." She could hear the weariness in her own voice.

"Heather, sorry to wake you. This is Jill Yates. I just got off the phone with Anne Braxton. She's absolutely frantic trying to find Ted Wirth. She was vague on the details, but there's some sort of emergency at the NIAR, and they need Ted. It must be big if they're calling me. I've got his phone number, but my call went straight to messaging, so he must have it turned off."

Yes, Ted turned off his phone before he went to bed so he wouldn't have to answer it at 3:34 a.m. Starting tonight, that would be Heather's new policy. "I'll see him in a few hours at work." Not technically a lie, just an omission. He was next to her in bed and starting to stir. She wasn't going to tell the woman whose name was on the foundation that she was sleeping with an underling. All the management books condemned the practice.

"That may not be good enough. I'll text his address. Is there any way you could drive there, wake him up, and have him call the number on the message I left on his cell phone? I would do it myself if I were there in San Diego, but I'm in Oregon."

Oh, sure you would, Jill. "I'll be happy to, Jill."

"Thank you. Like I said, I don't know what it's about, but it must be important. Have a nice day."

"You, too." She hung up. Ted looked at her inquisitively. "I'm supposed to drive to your apartment and tell you to call Jill Yates. Check your phone; she left a message with a number to call. There's a big emergency, and the NIAR needs you."

Ted's phone was on the nightstand on his side of her bed. He picked it up, turned it on, and checked his messages. He started dialing.

"What are you doing?"

"Dialing the number on Jill Yates's message."

"Not now! You have to wait the thirty or forty minutes it would take for me to drive to your apartment."

"I'm a little groggy at three thirty in the morning. Cobwebs."

Heather smiled. "Well, tall, dark, and handsome—"

"Distinguished. Once you hit a certain age, it's distinguished, not handsome."

"Well, tall, dark, and distinguished, seeing as how we're both up and we've got some time to kill…"

They hadn't given Ted all his degrees for nothing. He rolled toward Heather on the bed, and she proceeded to clear away his cobwebs.

His day off to a rousing, if early, start, Ted dialed Yates's number.

"Hello. Is this Ted Wirth?"

"It is."

"I'm glad Heather was able to get in touch with you. I guess you leave your phone off at night."

"I do."

"Ted, everything that I say and everything that you see and do from here on out has to remain strictly confidential. You can't tell anyone, including Heather or anyone else at the foundation. Do you understand?"

"Yes, Ms. Yates."

"Please, it's Jill."

"Okay, Jill."

"You first discovered the prime hormone factor, and your team researched it before the project was moved to the NIAR—"

"You mean before the NIAR hijacked it."

"Call it what you will, but don't let any resentment you might feel about that interfere with what I'm going to ask you to do. This is a matter of the gravest national importance. The NIAR needs your expertise—now. What's the earliest you can go to Washington?"

"This morning."

"Is nine too early?"

"No."

"Good. My private jet is already in the air from Portland and will be waiting for you at the San Diego Airport. I'll text you instructions on where to go and how to deal with security, and there'll be transportation waiting for you in Washington. Thank you, Ted." She hung up.

The look on Heather's face was a question.

"I'm flying to Washington this morning. You're not supposed to know that. You're not supposed to know anything. Since this is the government telling Jill Yates telling me to keep quiet, I'm going to tell you everything. It sounds like I'll be meeting with people at the NIAR. She said it was a matter of the 'gravest national importance.' It's got something to do with the Methuselah mice and PHF. I suppose I'll find out what when I get there."

She nodded. "We have to be very careful. Don't communicate with me from Washington."

"No, I won't."

The two men who met Ted at Dulles after he got off the jet looked like FIB or Secret Service agents: dark suits, heavy black rubber-soled shoes, earphones with wires that disappeared into their jackets, and sunglasses, although the terminal was brightly lit.

"I hope you had a pleasant flight, Dr. Wirth," one of the agents said, correctly polite, not extending his hand for a handshake. "We'll be taking you to your meeting. I'm Mr. Brahms, and my colleague is Mr. Sorenson. Your luggage has already been taken care of."

"You're with the NIAR?"

They didn't answer. Ted understood. The emergency that had brought him so quickly to Washington was going to involve the capital's netherworld of secrets, skullduggery, security, and intelligence, a world where questions were discouraged, answers were only for those who needed to know, and everyone else was kept in the dark. Nothing could have excited his curiosity more.

He was escorted out of the terminal to the departure drop-off area, where two black SUVs waited in a no-parking zone. Sorenson opened the front passenger door of the lead SUV for him, closed the door, went around the vehicle, and slid into the driver's seat. Brahms sat in the back seat.

"Dr. Wirth, I'll be your driver while you're in Washington." Sorenson started the car and pulled away from the curb.

Ted glanced in the rearview mirror. They were followed by the other SUV. Ted had never been an "important" person before: flying in a private plane, officially met and greeted when he arrived, his luggage taken care of, a driver. Could he get used to it, take it as his due, like a real Washington potentate? He hoped not. He didn't ask where they were going. After clearing the Dulles complex, they proceeded northwest, all three men silent, the only noise Brahms tapping out texts on his phone.

After about an hour, they turned off a highway onto an unmarked two-lane road. In ten minutes they came to a guard station in front of an ugly three-story beige box, surrounded by a tall chain link fence with barbed wire on top. Sorenson flashed a badge and the gate swung open. They parked in back of the building and entered it through a door that required an access card. Brahms navigated them through a maze of corridors and an elevator ride before he stopped in front of a door with a sign on it, *Conference Room A*. He opened the door. Five people sat at a rectangular table. Brahms motioned for Ted to enter, but he stayed in the hall and closed the door. Ted took the one empty chair, at the near end of the table. Before him sat a thin stack of papers on top of a loose-leaf binder, and a pen.

"Good afternoon, Dr. Wirth," said the man at the opposite end of the table. "Before we begin, you must read and sign the form at the top of the stack."

The form was a nondisclosure agreement, which stated that all documents and discussions in this meeting concerned matters of national security, required the highest level of confidentiality, and could not be disclosed. It warned Ted that should he do so, the full weight of twelve cited provisions, and possibly others, of the United States Criminal Code would come down upon him, and threatened penalties up to life in a maximum-security prison for even the tiniest of infractions. Apprehensive, he signed and dated the form.

"Dr. Wirth, I'm Dr. Earl Y. Graves. It was my decision to transfer your research project here to the National Institute of Aging Research. You weren't particularly happy about that decision."

"No, I wasn't."

"Quite understandable, but perhaps when you learn what has transpired since then, your feelings will change."

"What has transpired since then?"

"Allow me to introduce you to four of the medical researchers who continued your work on the project." He motioned to his left. "Dr. Jessica Randall and Dr. Matthew Vorhees. On the other side of the table, Dr. Gerald Michelson and Dr. Albert Gonzales. Jessica, why don't you bring Dr. Wirth up to speed?"

Dr. Randall, in her midfifties, wearing prim wire-framed glasses, her short black hair in a utilitarian bob, looked every inch the medical researcher. All that was missing was the white lab coat. "Thank you, Dr. Graves. When we assumed control of the project, our primary research focus was how to transfer what your team at Jill Yates had done in mice to human beings. We encountered the problems you had encountered. PHF, as you named it, occurs only in trace amounts in the roughly eighteen- to twenty-four-year age subset of the human population, and it's highly unstable outside the human body. However, we had one breakthrough. By a brute trial and error process, we discovered a chemical marker for PHF, a synthetic organic compound, dichlorophenincarboaxylate—or, as we call it, DCPC. Its chemical structure is described, in some detail, in your binder.

"This breakthrough allowed us to identify PHF in blood extracted from the human body. From that, we discovered that PHF starts deteriorating almost immediately upon extraction, which makes it both difficult and impractical to synthesize. For any life-extension therapy based on PHF to work, it would have to be quickly identified and transfused to an appropriately blood-matched recipient individual."

"But there's only a minute amount in any one donor's body. I would think you would have to essentially drain a donor's blood to get enough, especially given the deterioration, to have any effect on the recipient. That would kill the donor."

"That's correct. Actually, the difficulties are even more substantial. Once the blood is transfused, the deterioration stops. However, we discovered that it takes the PHF from more than one donor before any antiaging effects are registered with the recipient. Our experimental sequence is detailed in your binder. We determined that for each recipient, the PHF from twelve to eighteen donors is required, depending on body weight and other physiological factors."

"You didn't actually kill the donors."

"Yes, we did," Randall replied flatly.

Holy shit, he was sitting in a room full of Nazi butchers—Mengeles! "How the hell could you do that?"

"That is why this is top secret, and why you signed that nondisclosure agreement, Dr. Wirth," Graves said, his voice eerily calm. "It should be obvious that our work has the highest level of support."

"Where did you find the donors? How were you able to conduct these kinds of experiments?"

"That has to remain confidential," Graves replied. "All you need to know is that after our preliminary findings concerning the quantities of PHF necessary for human antiaging efficacy, an experiment was conducted at a remote but hospitable location. Dr. Michelson and Dr. Gonzales coordinated the NIAR effort."

"We had a donor population of roughly eleven hundred and sixty-nine recipients," Gonzales explained. "The results were—"

"You killed eleven hundred people?"

"Yes. As I was saying before you interrupted, the results were outstanding." He was being upbraided for being impolite by someone who had killed eleven hundred people! "Every single recipient demonstrated antiaging on every medical metric. We estimated the age reversal at between twenty and twenty-five years."

Mengeles! Mengeles! Mengeles! These people were discussing murder as they would an interesting specimen in a petri dish. "Why did you bring me here? I want no part of it."

"Something has gone horribly wrong," Graves said. "To be perfectly honest, you're a top-tier researcher and you got the ball rolling on this. I think when you hear what's gone wrong, you'll want to help, to save lives."

"Nine of the sixty-nine recipients have died," Michelson said. "They start vomiting and running fevers, and within a few days their systems fail completely. There are patient chronologies in your binder. We've been stymied trying to figure out either why they're dying or how to prevent it."

"From both a medical and a humanitarian point of view," Graves said, "we must try to save the lives of the remaining recipients. We need your help. Will you work with us?"

Ted knew he wasn't getting anything close to the full truth. They had killed eleven hundred; they wouldn't be this concerned with another sixty. They would let them die and chalk it up as a failed experiment if that were all there was to it. There was much more. Many lives, important lives, were on the line. But he wouldn't say anything about that. What to do? Play dumb, refuse to help, leave them with the consequences?

He could play dumb, he could refuse to help, but he couldn't leave them—he was basically their prisoner. They could hold him incommunicado for as long as they wanted. Ostensibly, nobody knew he was here. The men in dark suits could lock him away. A dismaying prospect, to be sure, but he had some leverage with the Mengeles: they needed him.

"I can't stand sitting in the same room with you and your people, Mr. Graves. Working with you would be out of the question. I'm not even going to call you 'doctor,' because doctors save lives; they don't intentionally kill people. I will devote my every effort to saving the lives of the remaining recipients—on my terms. I'll do the research in San Diego, at the Jill Yates Foundation, with the research team that worked on the project originally and with the administrative support of Heather Lindholm. We'll sign any NDA you want and work with whatever level of security you think appropriate. You'll have to inform Jill Yates so the necessary arrangements can be made and we get the resources we need. We'll have to have full access to all your research and experimental data. There are to be no repercussions if we're not successful. You can lock me up in a maximum-security prison, Mr. Graves, but those are my conditions. Take 'em or leave 'em."

"I don't have the authority to accept those conditions."

"Then you'd better find somebody who does. Time's a-wastin.'"

Ted was on Jill Yates's jet back to San Diego that evening. His team's work on the PHF antidote would begin the next day.

CHAPTER 17

DECEPTION

For many years the shepherd had tended his sheep and goats over the same pastures in central Syria. Compared to the rest of Syria, it was a good place to be. There was no oil or cities, so soldiers and marauding gangs mostly stayed away. Though other nations had sent their armies and machines of war to Syria, the area had remained relatively undisturbed, until the terrible gas attacks on the three villages.

The shepherd's world was simple. A few people in his village had radios or cell phones. From that limited contact with the outside world, he had learned that there had been big battles in central Syria, with many nations, gases from the sky, massive destruction, and deaths in the thousands. It was a terrible thing indeed.

Except the battles never happened.

Soldiers, mostly Syrians but some from other countries, patrolled the supposed battlefields in their jeeps and armored trucks, keeping people away by warning that it was dangerous because of the gases, which lingered and could still kill. They enforced their warnings with rifle fire when necessary. If it was so dangerous, why didn't the soldiers wear gas masks? The shepherd had slipped through the patrols, taking his flock to pastures inside the area patrolled. His goats and sheep grazed with no ill effects. He saw no burned-out vehicles, camps, helicopters, or planes, no bomb craters or rubble, no dead animals or people, no vultures or jackals feasting on carcasses. The land the shepherd roamed was the same as it was before the "battles."

He tried to tell the villagers what he had not seen. They would not come with him when he offered to show them. There might still be deadly gases. Why would the government say there were if there weren't? Why would it say there were battles if there were no battles? They would not trade with him—his sheep and goats might be poisoned by the gases. He argued with them, but they stopped listening. They said he was foolish, a crazy old man.

⋏

Carlos Valencia had checked Maplesville's phone book and public records. There was no listing or record of a Jasper Hewitt. Suspected government troll ProudAmerican had said that Jasper Hewitt had been wounded in central Syria and resided in Maplesville, Alabama. Carlos made phone calls to businesses there. None of the people he reached had heard of Hewitt. The population of the town was less than a thousand; somebody would have known him. ProudAmerican had been stupid to place his fake wounded soldier in such a small town, but stupidity was unsurprising from a government troll.

He had called veterans hospitals all over the country, trying to find warriors wounded in the terrible central Syrian battles. Tedious work, but rewarding for what he didn't find: a single wounded warrior from central Syria. He was onto something with this story, something big. First it had been the videos supposedly shot in Syria that were actually shot in Iraq in 2004. Now the absence of wounded, although in every other military engagement in the Middle East, the wounded outnumbered the dead.

Then there were the comments from Leonard Elkington and other relatives of soldiers killed in central Syria, their inability to get a list of those who had died. Today, Carlos was going to wade into the Department of Defense bureaucracy and try to get either the list or a reason why it was not being made public. He checked the time on his computer: seven forty-five. Washington was an hour ahead; he'd start calling in fifteen minutes. He'd already sent an e-mail to the Defense Department's Public Web Help Desk, expecting not even a remotely helpful answer. It might take up most of the morning, navigating through automated-voice-messaging-system mazes because he fell into that dreaded category—callers unaware of their parties' extensions, dropped calls, and the occasional voice of a real-life, albeit completely unhelpful, human. However, it was necessary for him to run the gauntlet, especially if, as expected, he got nothing from it. He sipped his coffee, a caffeine boost for the coming tedium.

"Dad, I've got it." Peter stood in the doorway. "You want to see?"

Carlos jumped from his chair. "You bet." They walked into Peter's room. Carlos sat down in front of Peter's computer. Peter stood behind him.

"Here's the list, Dad. There are two thousand one hundred forty-two people. This took a lot of hacking. It's at the highest level of security, right up there with nuclear secrets. They don't want anybody to see this."

"How did you get in?"

"If I told you, I'd have to kill you."

A joke! His son told a joke! It was an old joke, a cliché joke, but it was a joke! Perhaps his second one that year. You cherished the milestones as they came.

"This is downloaded. I did the actual searching for the list on another computer, with a fake name and password. I'm not sure if you should know more."

"I'm not sure I should, either. Any chance you'll get caught?"

"Very low probability. I exercised extreme caution."

Carlos examined the list, a chart on a spreadsheet. The names of the dead were in alphabetical order in the first column. He saw Aubrey Elkington's name. There were ten other columns: Social Security number, sex, ethnicity, rank, dates of birth and death, cause of death, hometown, an X indicating the body had been recovered, and an X indicating it had been shipped to the United States. "Can you print this out?"

"Yes, but it will be a lot of pages."

"That's okay. I just want a hard copy. You keep a USB drive. Destroy it if the Feds are at the door, and I'll burn the hard copy."

"There's something interesting here."

"Besides the fact that all the bodies have been recovered and shipped back home? Nobody blown up so bad their body couldn't be either recovered or identified?"

"That's explainable. This could be just a list of the known dead because their bodies were recovered. It says at the top: *Central Syria Dead.* There may be others who haven't been found who aren't accounted for, so they didn't make the list. I'm talking about something else." Peter often missed what was obvious to everyone else, but picked up obscure details everyone else overlooked. He would point out a background actor making a fleeting appearance in a movie or TV show who was the same background actor who had made a fleeting appearance in some other movie or TV show, years earlier. "Look at the dates of birth. They all fall within a six-year range. All the dead were eighteen to twenty-four years old."

"That makes sense. That's the usual age of soldiers."

"Enlisted, low-ranking soldiers, but not officers. You have this huge war, lots of countries involved, bombing and heavy artillery, chemical and biological agents, but the only ones killed are in that age range. Look at the rank column. They're all lower ranks. Not one older officer. Officers die in wars. How could they not die in this one? Gases don't discriminate between ranks."

"Maybe they're on a different list."

"If they are, I couldn't find it."

"Did you look for a list of the wounded?"

"I couldn't find that either, or a list of the missing. This is the only list I found."

Carlos needed to think. "Print a copy for me." He rose, walked back to his study, and sat down in his chair in front of his computer. He would have to tiptoe on this next article. Stating that he had called most of the nation's veterans hospitals and had been unable to contact anyone who had been wounded in central Syria wouldn't raise red flags. Assuming the government checked—always the prudent assumption—they would discover from his phone records that he had indeed called the hospitals.

The tricky part was how much he could reveal from the list. There was no way he could say that the dead fell in a six-year age range, or that all the bodies had been found and sent home, without revealing to the government that he had seen its top secret, highest-security list. All he could do was spend the morning on the phone with the Department of Defense, getting nowhere, as he had planned.

The article he would write would raise questions and suspicions but offer no conclusions. He just had to make sure that it didn't put him and Peter in jail.

CHAPTER 18

A PLAN

Sometimes in his medical research, disparate elements came together all at once, producing a breakthrough. Ted was having a breakthrough moment as he read an article on the Internet, but it had nothing to do with his medical research.

"Holy shit, you've got to see this," he said to Heather. He had cooked her dinner at his apartment and she was cleaning up. She came to his desk. He slid out of his chair so she could sit down and read what he had just read, an article from the website NoneoftheAbove.com, Carlos Valencia's blog.

> *Long-time readers know my philosophy about anything from the government: it's a lie until proven otherwise. In "Syria Looks a Lot like Iraq," I posted a series of videos purportedly from the battles in central Syria that were identical to videos on the Internet that were purportedly from Iraq in 2004. The videos elicited some heated discussion, but the provenance of either set was never conclusively and satisfactorily established. Despite a request for comments, the government has said nothing about them.*

Heather clicked a link to the earlier story and watched the two sets of videos. She clicked back to Valencia's article.

Certain aspects of the central Syrian situation seem odd to me, and I have continued to investigate. After the Grand Coulee Dam disaster and the chemical/biological attacks on the three Syrian villages, US allies and opponents quickly escalated their involvement in Syria. The fighting, which had primarily been in western, northern, and northeastern Syria, moved to the desert in central Syria, with widespread carnage and massive casualties taken by all sides, far greater than in previous Syrian battles. Chemical and biological agents were used, but it has not been determined conclusively to what extent or who introduced them into the battles.

Over two thousand US troops lost their lives, and the total death toll approached twenty thousand. Chemical and biological agents have rendered a wide swath of central Syria uninhabitable, and media and civilians have been barred from the area. A few selected members of the media have been able to fly over it in helicopters, and they have reported on the death and destruction, although they have not been permitted to take pictures because of the area's continuing military sensitivity.

A reader of my earlier article, Leonard Elkington, whose daughter Aubrey died in the Syrian battles, commented that he had been unable to obtain a list of all those who had died there. I have made an exhaustive effort to find the list Mr. Elkington could not obtain. We may have talked to the same people within the Department of Defense.

Unfortunately, my result has been the same as his. The department, if it has a list of those who died in the terrible Syrian battles, will not release it. I have made multiple requests, over the telephone, via e-mails, and even in a letter delivered certified mail, and have been refused every time (except for the letter, which was never answered). At the same time, I have received no official confirmation that the department will not release the list. There is no obvious explanation why it will not do so.

Strange, even suspicious, as this seems, it pales in comparison to my investigation into the "wounded" of Syria. Simply put, I have found none. Generally in battle, the wounded are a multiple of the dead. Presumably the Syrian wounded would have been transported back to the United States and received treatment at military and veterans hospitals. However, I called virtually every facility in this country and have been unable to make contact with anyone who was wounded.

So we have videos of a war that are identical to videos that may have been taken over a decade earlier, in a different war. From battles so terrible that only a few are permitted to view its aftermath, the government will not provide the names of those killed, and apparently nobody was wounded. In a matter this sensitive, I hate to draw any conclusion other than that something doesn't add up. Fortunately, the conflict in Syria appears to have subsided back to what it was before the big battles. It's impossible not to wonder what actually happened during those battles, or whether they even occurred.

Heather looked up at Ted, standing behind her. "It's almost too terrible to think about."

"That's where our plutocrats got their donors. Twelve to eighteen per plutocrat. Over twenty thousand died; that would be at least eleven hundred of the world's highest and mightiest who received those kids' PHF. Maybe more."

"You know why they won't release the names? Somebody would notice that all the dead fall within a six-year age range."

"Sacrifice the young so a bunch of bastards can cheat death and hold on to their money and power and perks. It's beyond criminal. It's monstrous, utterly depraved, worse than war. And these are the people running the world. We should quit our research right now and let them all die."

Heather shook her head. "There are still those first recipients, the poor guinea pigs, whoever and wherever they are. They don't deserve to die."

⊼

Under different circumstances, Ted and Heather would have held hands and strolled through Balboa Park's eclectic and magnificent collection of gardens. Today they would be strolling, but holding hands would be out of the question, and they wouldn't be enjoying the botanical displays.

Yesterday, Heather had given all the members of the research team the same handwritten note.

Team meeting at 7:00 p.m. tomorrow at Balboa Park, Botanical Building by the Lily Pond. Change clothes before you come—casual or athletic—with comfortable shoes. Do not bring any type of electronics. Destroy this note.

The team members assumed that everywhere they went, every phone call, Internet search, and e-mail sent or received, was monitored by the government. They assumed that every conference room, office, and lab, the hallways, and maybe even the bathrooms at the Jill Yates Foundation were bugged, as well as their apartments and houses. The government might be listening to their conversations through their smartphones and mobile computers. Ted and Heather assumed the government knew about their affair. So be it. They were living in a fishbowl, but fish had to mate now and then.

The ever-watchful government would, in its surveillance of the team members, discover the team meeting that evening at Balboa Park. Sometimes fish had to meet and confer, too, hang the surveillance. The meeting couldn't be kept secret, but Ted and Heather had decided that if the group talked as it strolled around the park, it was their best chance for keeping the conversation from the government. The only bugs on the plants would be the live variety, and the team would see any would-be eavesdroppers.

Terri Gibson was the first member of the team to join Ted and Heather at the designated meeting place. She had been unable to find a job after Heather had to let her go. In the search for a cure, Heather knew the foundation would deny her nothing. Teri's reinstatement was her first request. The other researchers, Alan, Linda, and Jack, arrived as a group a few minutes later, followed by Carl, the lab technician.

"The team's all here," Ted said. "Let's go this way." He pointed toward the Casa del Rey Moro Garden, done in the style of a Moorish garden in Spain. They meandered by a wishing well and numerous tourists and soon found an isolated, shaded walkway. Birds chirped, bees buzzed, flowers were in bloom, and mingled scents filled the air. They stopped at a spot offering a sweeping prospect of a ravine below, ostensibly enjoying the lush view.

"Heather and I believe that we have been asked to develop a PHF antidote for many more people than we've been told about. It stands to reason, with all the rush-rush and top secret we're going through, that there's substantially more at stake than the lives of the test subjects who are still alive. We think that PHF was transfused into eleven to sixteen hundred of the world's most powerful and wealthy people."

The group was stunned, silent.

"All Americans?" Jack finally asked.

"No, from around the world."

"But that would require fifteen to twenty thousand donors," Terri said. "How could they kill that many young people and get away with it, without anybody noticing?"

"Battles that weren't battles. There's a blog, NoneoftheAbove.com, written by a guy named Carlos Valencia. Don't hop on your computers to check the site out; the government will get suspicious. He's posted two articles. He claims that government videos from the central Syrian battles are actually from Iraq and were taken in 2004. He also claims he's called all the military and veterans hospitals and has been unable to find a single person who was wounded in central Syria. Finally, he says the government won't release a list of those who were killed."

"Are you saying that the government staged central Syria? That's how it got the donors?" Linda asked.

"Not just our government. Russia, Syria, the Arab monarchies, Turkey, Iran, Iraq, and our allies in Europe. They all played a part. They agreed to help stage it, and our government gave their head honchos the fountain of youth."

"That would explain why nobody can get into the area where the fighting supposedly took place," Alan said.

Heather nodded toward a large group approaching them. They strolled out of the Moorish park down a trail toward the Japanese Friendship Garden.

"If Syria was staged," Jack said, "then what led up to it was probably staged—the dam and the massacre of those villages."

"I hope the massacre was staged, that it didn't really happen," Heather replied. "We know the dam happened; you can't fake that. But it might have been our government, not Egyptian terrorists, who did it. There was a video Ted and I saw on the Internet. You can't find it any—"

The members of the group glanced at each other.

"Why are you looking like that? Is there some secret I'm not in on?

"Uh, we know you and Ted are seeing each other, Heather," Linda replied.

"It's hard to keep things from the people you work with. I"—Heather glanced at Ted—"*we* would appreciate it if this could stay within our group."

"Absolutely."

"Thank you. Now the video—it was supposedly taken at the dam. It shows the jet crashing into it and then another much larger explosion a second or two later, some distance from the first. In addition, I put together a kind of before-and-after file of pictures of prominent people who suddenly appeared to look younger."

They stopped talking as they passed a group of Japanese tourists taking pictures of themselves in front of the same flora they had back home.

"So now we're faced with an ethical question," Heather said. "We of course want to develop an antidote for the remaining test patients, but in so doing, we're also going to be saving the lives of people who have done something unconscionable and terrible. They've murdered people just so they could extend their own lives. Ted and I didn't feel like we could do that without discussing it with you and asking what you think about it."

There was a long silence, which Linda broke.

"Even if the lives of the test subjects weren't at stake, I don't think we can refuse to develop an antidote just because it will keep bad people alive. That's playing God, not a role I'm comfortable playing. We might be able to expose what they did, if we're willing to run the risk. Maybe they'd be brought to justice, but we can't be the judge, jury, and executioner."

"Well put," Alan said. "Nothing's saying we'll even come up with an antidote, but if we do, I think we have to make sure somehow that only we know how to produce it. Or maybe only one of us—Ted probably—knows from soup to nuts how to produce it. We can't let them think they can get away with it next time because they can make their own antidote."

"If we develop an antidote, we'll have the lives of the most important people in the world in our hands," Jack said. "Talk about leverage! Think of what we could ask for."

"It would be entirely wrong to use this situation for personal gain," Linda said.

"Leverage, leverage," Ted said, excited. "Not for personal gain or anything like that, but as Jack said, we have leverage. Here's an idea…"

For the next forty-five minutes, the group wandered through different gardens, not paying much attention to where they were going or who might be listening. The "meeting" was adjourned after they had thoroughly discussed Ted's idea and devised a plan.

CHAPTER 19

TERRORISTS

The doorbell was ringing. Carlos stirred, awoke, and sat up groggily in bed. Anita was still asleep. He went to the closet and put on his bathrobe and slippers. The doorbell rang again. He left the bedroom, stepped down the stairs, went to the front door, and peered through the peephole. Two men in dark suits stood on the doorstep.

"Who are you?"

"Agents Mulroney and Rose, from the Federal Investigations Bureau. May we please enter?"

Carlos felt a cold sensation in his stomach and tightness in his throat and chest. "Do you have a warrant?"

"Yes, we do. Please open the door."

Carlos opened the door.

"I'm Agent Mulroney, and this is Agent Rose."

"Can I see your warrant?"

Mulroney handed him two documents. The top of the first read: *Special Domestic Terrorism Court.* It was a warrant for his arrest and a search of the premises: *United States of America, Plaintiff, v. Carlos Ernesto Valencia, Defendant.* Carlos checked the second document: *United States of America, Plaintiff, v. Peter Michael Valencia, Defendant.* No, no, it couldn't be, not his son. They could take him, but not Peter. The poor kid would be terrified. If he went to jail, the other prisoners would chew him up. This couldn't be happening.

Anita came down the stairs. "What's going on?"

"I'm being arrested, and they're arresting Peter, too." His voice was shaky.

"For what?"

"Inciting domestic terrorism," Mulroney replied. "I assume you're Mrs. Valencia?"

Anita nodded.

"Would you please get your son?"

Her eyes went wide. "You can't arrest Peter. What's he done?"

"Dear, go get him or they will."

She went up the stairs followed by Agent Rose. Carlos and Mulroney stood silently, waiting. In a few minutes Anita and Rose reappeared with Peter, his face drained white with confusion and fear.

"Peter, don't be afraid," Carlos said. "This is all a mistake. Don't say anything to these agents, or anyone else from the government, until you talk to our lawyer."

Peter nodded. He was dressed in street clothes, reminding Carlos he was in his pajamas and bathrobe, hardly what he wanted to wear to either a court or detention facility. "I need to change my clothes."

"I'll go with you," Mulroney said.

They went upstairs to the bedroom. Carlos dressed while the agent stood outside the door. Carlos glanced at the clock on the nightstand: *2:47.* Why were he and Peter being arrested at this hour? He went back downstairs with the agent.

"Before we go wherever we're going, can Anita make a copy of your warrants?"

"No," Mulroney replied.

"Where are we going?"

"I'm not at liberty to say."

"Anita, call Fred and Harold," Carlos said. Fred Cunningham was his lawyer and Harold Sayers his best friend.

Rose handed Anita a document, let her look at it for a few seconds, and then took it back. "Mrs. Valencia, you are hereby under a Special Domestic Terrorism Court order not to reveal to anyone that the Federal Investigations Bureau was here tonight or that your husband and son were arrested. After we leave, an FIB search team will enter your house and conduct a search. You are not to reveal that search or the nature of any items the FIB confiscates. Failure to comply with this order will result in an arrest warrant from the SDTC and your incarceration."

After he had posted his last article on central Syria, Carlos had made Peter give him the USB drive with the list of the war dead. It was too hot to keep. He had destroyed the drive and his own paper list. Now he was relieved he had done so, but wondered whether it would make a difference. Whatever was going to happen to him and Peter didn't look as if it was going to be in accordance with normal arrest or judicial procedures...or the US Constitution. If Anita couldn't talk, how was he going to notify his attorney? Maybe that was the point of the gag order. What was this Special Domestic Terrorism Court? He had never heard of it.

Carlos's seven-year-old daughter, Denise, came down the stairs, rubbing her sleepy eyes. "Daddy, who are these men in black? What's happening?"

Anita put an arm on Denise's shoulder. "These men need to talk to your father and Peter. They're going to go with them, but they'll be back."

"When?"

"I don't know, but soon."

Denise stared at Rose and Mulroney. "They're bad men, mommy." She started to cry.

"Mr. Valencia, if you and your son will come with us," Rose said.

Denise rushed to Carlos and he hugged her, wondering when he'd hug her again. Anita embraced Peter.

"This is illogical, Mom."

Rose motioned for Carlos and Peter to follow him, and Mulroney brought up the rear. Anita hugged her husband and pried Denise away from him. Denise saw her mother crying and her wailing intensified. The only other time Carlos had felt this distressed and horrified was when, as a thirteen-year-old, he had shouted at his little brother, who was chasing the family dog into the street. He watched helplessly as his little brother and the dog were run over and killed. His eyes filled with tears.

Why weren't they being handcuffed? Was it out of concern for the feelings of his wife and daughter? Get real. Everything about this arrest was designed to further its secrecy. Handcuffs might have alerted any neighbors watching the early morning scene that Carlos and Peter were being arrested. Sinister…very sinister.

Two black SUVs waited at the curb. Carlos was led to the first one and Peter the second.

"Can Peter and I ride together?"

"No," Rose replied.

"Don't say a word, Peter." Carlos knew he wouldn't. Peter followed directions, sometimes to the point of absurdity. He wouldn't tell the agents he had to go to the bathroom even if his bladder was bursting.

They drove to the multiblock complex of federal buildings in downtown Austin, not far from the Texas State Capitol, and parked in an underground lot. Waiting for them were four agents, who joined the two agents in Carlos's SUV and the two agents in Peter's SUV and escorted the group through a maze of hallways and stairs. Carlos tried to stay close to Peter, hoping his presence would offer some reassurance. The technuman looked like a death row inmate on his last walk. They stopped at a room with a sign on the door: *Interrogation Room.*

"Peter, please," one of the agents said, opening the door. Peter looked at his father, and Carlos shook his head. "He won't say anything without a lawyer present. Don't say anything, Peter."

Peter and three of the agents went into the interrogation room. The other agents and Carlos went down the hall to another interrogation room. Carlos entered it with Rose, Mulroney, and another agent. Carlos sat on one side of a rectangular table. The three agents sat on the other side. Carlos wondered whether the dark glass behind them shielded agents in an adjacent room.

"Mr. Valencia, I'm Agent Steadman of the Federal Investigations Bureau. I believe you know Agents Rose and Mulroney. We'll be conducting your questioning."

"You haven't read me or Peter the Miranda warning, but I assure you I'm not saying a thing without a lawyer present."

"Mr. Valencia, the Miranda warning is required in criminal proceedings. You have been arrested under Executive Order 13905, which governs procedures for domestic terrorism, pursuant to the president's powers under the National Defense Authorization Act. You and your son are prisoners in the war against terrorism. As such, your constitutional criminal rights are inapplicable. EO 13905 specifies that your case must be reviewed by the Special Domestic Terrorism Court prior to your apprehension, but once it has been determined that it is more likely than not that you have engaged in domestic terrorism, you can be detained indefinitely without being charged and without legal counsel."

Carlos felt as if someone were taking a sledgehammer to his chest. This couldn't be America. Not the America his grandfather, an immigrant from Guatemala, had told him about so proudly when he was a boy. Not the America that had made the day of his naturalization ceremony the happiest day of his life. Not the America of freedom and opportunity, where you didn't have to bribe someone just to make a living, where the government couldn't throw you in jail on a whim. This wasn't America.

"So we're here because a court set up by the president has decided we're terrorists. Nobody is to know we're here. I can't contact a lawyer, and you can hold us here as long as you want."

"Mr. Valencia, you are suspected of waging war against your government and are being treated accordingly. Prisoners of war do not enjoy the rights afforded to criminals. You and your son's treatment will be governed by the third Geneva Convention."

"How do we get out of here?"

Steadman smiled. "Now we're getting somewhere. You can start by telling us how you—or more accurately, your computer-genius son—got the videos of Iraq from classified government archives. And what led you to publicly question the veracity of the official accounts of the war in Syria?"

There was hope. The videos had been hacked from the government and they suspected Peter, but they didn't know how he had done it. And Steadman hadn't said anything about the far more damaging list of dead Peter had hacked, so they might not even know about that. Damn, his kid was smart; maybe he really had covered his tracks. What they appeared most upset about was that Carlos had questioned their story, which meant that story was a lie—a big one. Which also meant that while hacking may have been the basis for the "domestic terrorism" charge, this drill might be less about that and more about intimidation. Perhaps they wanted to shut him up rather than lock him up. That was the hope.

"I'm not saying a word until I have a lawyer, and Peter won't either."

"Then you and Peter will be the government's guests in a federal detention facility."

⋏

It was too early in the morning to call Carlos's attorney, so Anita called his best friend, Harold Sayers.

"Hello," Harold answered, yawning.

"Harold, I'm sorry to wake you up, but something terrible has happened. Carlos and Peter have been arrested."

"Arrested? Arrested…by whom?"

"The FIB, working under something called the Special Domestic Terrorism Court. Have you ever heard of that? About an hour ago they arrested them and wouldn't say where they were taking them."

"I never heard of that court. Can you give me a few minutes to get a cup of coffee? I'll call you right back."

"Sure. Thanks."

Five minutes later, he called. "Anita, I'm at my desk. What was the name of that court? I'll do a search on it."

"The Special Domestic Terrorism Court."

"Here it is. It was set up by an executive order, pursuant to the National Defense Authorization Act. A court set up by the president—there goes the Constitution, that's a legislative function. According to this summary, it basically changes the treatment of US citizens suspected of terrorism to that of foreign citizens suspected of terrorism. They're prisoners of war, not criminals with rights. This is outrageous. How the hell did it get through? They can hold Carlos and Peter indefinitely without legal process."

"What do we do?"

"It looks like they're doing their best to keep everything secret. Our best hope is probably publicity. Can you get on Carlos's Internet site? That's publicity the government can't control."

"I don't know how to do that."

"You need to get on his computer. Hopefully you won't need a password. Go into his browser history—"

"Wait a minute, let me write this down. 'Browser history.'"

"You'll see his site name with something like the word 'administrator' with it. Click that link. It may require a password to log in, but if we're lucky, since Carlos posts so much, he clicked a box saying something like 'Keep me logged in,' and the username and password will autofill. If it does, you'll go to a page that will let you post on his site. Or you might be able to bypass the log-in entirely and go straight to the posting screen."

"Okay, let me see if I got this. Administrator, log in, autofill, and then post. What do I write for my post?"

"Just say what happened, that Carlos and Peter were arrested by the FIB, and make sure you mention this special court."

"The FIB gave me a gag order. I'm not supposed to talk about this, to disclose the arrest, or I can be arrested."

"Anita, I don't know what else can be done. Any public disclosure and the FIB will know it originated with you."

There was a long silence. "You know I'd do anything for Carlos and Peter. If I get arrested, will you and Carol take care of Denise?"

"Of course. I just thought of something. You'd better hurry, because they might shut down Carlos's website."

"Right. What if I can't get on?"

"Call me back and we'll figure out something else."

"Bye."

Anita was able to post on NoneoftheAbove.com.

Today at around 3:00 a.m., two men from the FIB arrested my husband, Carlos Valencia, and my son, Peter, at our house. Their arrests were authorized by the Special Domestic Terrorism Court. This same court issued a gag order ordering me not to disclose the arrests, saying I would be arrested if I did. The FIB agents would not say where Carlos and Peter were being taken. They drove away in two black SUVs. I have not heard from them, although they are supposed to have the right to make a phone call. If I comply with the terms of the gag order, I will not be able to contact an attorney.

This is not a joke or a prank. Everything has happened exactly as I say here. If you value Carlos, and more importantly, if you value civil liberties and your rights, please repost this and send it to all your e-mail contacts. The government cannot be allowed to act in this unlawful way. Thank you.

Within an hour of her post, NoneoftheAbove.com experienced a mysterious malfunction and went dark. Within another hour, Anita had been arrested. By the end of the day, her post had gone viral from readers who had reposted it and sent it to their e-mail contacts before the site went dark. "Special Domestic Terrorism Court" was one of the day's top search-engine searches.

CHAPTER 20

ANTIDOTE

It had taken almost two months of round-the-clock effort, but the team was on the verge of a breakthrough. Along the way, they had made discoveries which revolutionized the science of aging in the human body, discoveries that would never be published in a medical research journal. The Magnificent Seven, the team's name for itself, watched a microscopic world on a computer screen. One chemical compound was absorbing another, destroying it. The absorbed compound was PHF. The absorbing compound Ted had christened anti-PHF.

"That's how it's supposed to work," Ted said. "That's how it does work absent any human interference during the normal aging process. Mother Nature is determined to deny us immortality. She gives us PHF for a few fleeting years, during our prime, but the PHF produces its own destroyer—anti-PHF—which kicks in about the age of twenty-four. Within a year it has done its job. Alan and Linda have discovered the problem with the test subjects—mutant anti-PHF. Mother Nature especially didn't like this NIAR effort."

"We're not sure," Alan said, "what produces mutant anti-PHF, or for brevity's sake, MAP. It could be that PHF degrades in the transfusion process, impairing its ability to make anti-PHF. Or it could be that PHF changes once it's inside the bodies of the recipient. Either way, it produces MAP rather than regular anti-PHF, and MAP is responsible for the recipients' gruesome deaths. MAP is especially virulent. It destroys not just PHF but most of the rest of the body's systems as well."

"Why didn't the NIAR discover anti-PHF or MAP?" Heather asked. The demonstration and explanation were for her benefit. She was not actively involved with the research, but she was the leader of the team and received regular updates.

"That's not the direction they went in their research," Alan answered. "They were looking at PHF, but didn't test to see if there might be other compounds at work. Anti-PHF is only found in trace amounts in the bodies of eighteen- to twenty-three-year olds. More of what is produced is produced when a person reaches twenty-four or twenty-five, usually enough to be detectable, but just barely. The increased level of anti-PHF production kicks in about six months before the anti-PHF absorbs PHF. MAP does its dirty work and vanishes. Monitoring still-healthy recipients of PHF, we found that MAP suddenly spikes up to a detectable quantity, destroys PHF and attacks the body's systems, causing the quick deaths. However, MAP disappears before the victim dies, and so is undetectable in the autopsy. It's no surprise the NIAR people didn't find it."

"So the task became how to develop a way to stop MAP," Ted said. "Terri and Jack did most of the work on that."

"Ted's being modest, he did quite a bit." Terri said. "We were able to extract enough MAP from one dying recipient to conduct NMR spectroscopy, which allowed us to determine its structure. From that, we've produced a compound that we believe will neutralize MAP. It should be durable enough that it can be injected before MAP spikes in a recipient's body."

"So you've produced anti-mutant-anti-prime-hormone-factor, or A-M-A-P-H-F?" Heather said. She smiled. Ted had loosened her up; she told the occasional joke now. "But if you neutralize MAP, does that mean that the PHF will still be in the recipients' bodies and they'll have extended lifespans?"

"No, we've configured what you call AMAPHF—we're just calling it the antidote—so that it not only destroys the mutation, it destroys the PHF.

That, at least, is what we believe will happen, but we need to test it on the initial recipients who are still alive."

"Last check with the NIAR, there were four. I'll arrange for you and Jack to go to Houston."

The NIAR had been particularly secretive about information concerning the test group of recipients. When members of Ted's team had required samples and tests from those recipients, they had flown to Houston and the recipients had been brought in from wherever they were located, which was never disclosed. All procedures were performed in the presence of NIAR monitors, who made sure the team members did not ask for, and the recipients did not divulge, sensitive information.

"If they're down to four, we'd better hurry," Jack said.

⋏

One month later, Ted allowed himself a sigh of relief. The four were still kicking. Terri and Jack had gone to Houston. Under the ever-watchful eyes of their NIAR monitors they had administered the antidote. They had taken only four vials and had thoroughly washed the empties, lest anyone from the NIAR contemplated reverse engineering the antidote from residual drops in the vials. Ted looked at a chart on his computer that Terri had just sent him. The antidote recipients' PHF levels were close to zero. This was the first confirmation that the antidote had not only stopped MAP, but that it was also destroying PHF. Unfortunately for the four recipients, they would live out only a normal life span. Fortunately for the world, so would the high and mighty who had received PHF…assuming they received the antidote.

Ted walked into Heather's office. "Did you see the chart from Terri?"

"Yes. The declining PHF levels mean the antidote is doing what it's supposed to do?"

"That's right. It's time for a phone call to the NIAR."

Heather put her speaker on and tapped a speed dial key. The other end rang several times.

"Jessica Randall."

"Hello, Jessica, it's Heather. I've got you on speakerphone and Ted is here."

"Good afternoon, Ted. It's been heartening to see that your latest treatment appears to be working. It's been a month and all four of the recipients are still alive."

"Thank you."

"Would you say that the efficacy of your antidote has been confirmed?"

"Yes, with the qualification that it's only been a month. There's always the possibility that something untoward could happen."

"Jessica," Heather said, "now that the team has developed the antidote and apparently saved the last PHF recipients' lives, it's time for a break. You know how hard everyone has worked on this...late nights and weekends. There are still a few loose ends, but once those are taken care of, we'd like to wrap this thing up, get our lives back on track."

There was a long silence. "Let me clear that with Doctor Graves. We'll get back to you."

Graves called Heather thirty minutes later. She put him on hold and summoned Ted to her office. "You're on speakerphone, Doctor Graves. Ted Wirth is here."

"I'll get right to it. You can't terminate your project just yet. We're going to need you to continue producing your antidote. We weren't entirely forthcoming about the number of recipients."

"I find it shocking that a group of killers would lie too."

"Call it what you will, Doctor Wirth. I don't have time for moralizing right now."

"You should try making time for it. How many doses of antidote do you need, Mr. Graves?"

There was a long silence. "About fourteen hundred." There was another long silence.

"And who might these fourteen hundred recipients be?"

"I'm not at liberty to divulge that. What I can tell you is that getting antidotes to these recipients is the highest national priority. Not doing so would have a devastating global impact."

"I've noticed many heads of state and other potentates seem to be looking more chipper lately, including our own beloved President Lochness. In fact, if I didn't know better, I'd say Washington's water supply has tapped into a fountain of youth."

"What you're implying is just conjecture."

"Well here's another conjecture. If you've got fourteen hundred recipients, that would mean you needed, at an average of fifteen per, twenty-one-thousand donors. What a coincidence, about that many died recently in Syria and they were in the right age cohort."

"I'm not conceding anything, but let's assume that what you're implying did indeed happen. Surely you can see how vital it is that we get the antidote?"

"We can," Heather said.

"Good. Production times will be greatly accelerated when you give us the formula for the antidote and we produce it here, in addition to your production out there."

"You're not getting that formula," Ted said.

"What do you mean we're not getting the formula?"

"Exactly what I said. You're not getting the formula. We'll produce it here."

"You realize you're risking the lives of the most important people in the world?"

"So that's not conjecture, after all."

Graves was silent. Finally he said, "You would risk their lives?"

"I would, and not feel particularly bad about it either, given what they've done. You're one of those important people, aren't you, Graves? It would be a pleasure not to produce the antidote for you, but don't worry, you'll get your dose if we can produce it on time. I'm the only person on our team who has the complete formula, so don't try anything stupid with the other members."

"That's how we agreed to set it up," Heather said, "so that only Mr. Wirth would have the entire formula."

"You're putting me in a very awkward position."

"That's your problem," Ted replied, "but not half as awkward as the one my other condition will put you in."

"What's that?"

"I want a meeting with Lochness, one-on-one. If I don't get it, no antidote."

"You know I can't grant you that."

"Then you'd better find somebody who can. We wouldn't want the most important people in the world to start dying off, now would we? Time's a wastin, Mr. Graves."

CHAPTER 21

NONNEGOTIABLE

Ted had never been in the White House. Most of his trips to Washington had been on business, and he hadn't had time to play tourist. The White House hadn't been at the top of his list on two trips when he was younger and had actually been a tourist. Now, after a hastily arranged trip on Jill Yates's jet, a reception at the airport by a phalanx of men in dark suits, and a ride into Washington amid a convoy of black SUVs, he was in the Oval Office.

Politicians were expert in arranging their facial expressions to suit their purposes, but today, President Lochness's face wasn't hiding his feelings: scared and pissed off. However, he did look younger.

"Help yourself from the coffee service, Dr. Wirth."

"Thank you, Mr. President, I believe I will."

Ted poured coffee from a silver pot into a bone china cup, placed it on a saucer with the presidential seal, and poured cream from a silver creamer. President Lincoln or one of the Roosevelts might have used this service. Everything in the White House, especially in the Oval Office, probably had some historical significance. Stepping around the Great Seal on the beige carpet, he returned to where he had been sitting on a dull, mustard-color couch across from the president and set his cup and saucer on the table between them.

"As you might have guessed, Dr. Wirth, I'm a busy man." The president smiled wanly. "Let's cut right to the chase. What do you want?"

Ted had mentally rehearsed his answer to that question all the way from San Diego. Still, he was nervous. The brusque abruptness, and that he was in the Oval Office with the president of the United States, threw him off balance. The president was probably counting on that. Steady. Remember, this was the man who had thousands of people killed so he and his pals could live longer.

"Mr. President, PHF reversed the aging process for you and fourteen hundred important people around the world. That procedure cost the lives of over twenty thousand donors. Those donors were members of the military of the United States and other nations. They were supposedly killed in battles in Syria, but they were really killed when their blood was drained from them for transfusions to the fourteen hundred recipients."

"I'm going to neither confirm nor deny what you're saying."

"You don't have to. My team wouldn't have received an urgent order for fourteen hundred doses of antidote and I wouldn't be sitting here if it weren't true. You don't want to confirm it, fine. I'll just assume you've found an amazing rejuvenation therapy and never received a PHF transfusion. If that's the case, we need not produce an antidote for you."

"Quit playing games, Wirth. What do you want?"

"You and the leadership of countries involved in the Middle East staged a fake war in Syria. It must have taken a tremendous amount of cooperation and coordination. That's inspiring. You staged your fake war, now I—*we*, the members of the team, want you and the other leaders to stage a real peace."

"Oh good God, that's idiotic! My predecessors and I have tried to bring peace to the Middle East for decades. What do you want me to do? We've tried diplomacy, intelligence, counterinsurgency, military solutions, regime change, winning hearts and minds. You want more conferences, more troops, more weapons, more money? Bring home more bodies? The American people are goddamn sick of the Middle East! They'll never stand for it, even if I could guarantee peace there, which I can't."

"None of the above. As you just said, nothing you've tried has worked. You've made things incalculably worse. It's time to try something different. We want a multinational withdrawal of all foreign military and intelligence forces from Morocco to Pakistan. No withdrawal, no antidote."

Lochness's expression was an amalgam of astonishment, rage, and fear. "I can't do that. Just up and leave? I'll never get it through Congress, or the other countries."

"Their leaders face the same choice you do, Mr. President—withdraw or die."

"You are out of your mind! Using my life as a bargaining chip for this change in policy, trying to pressure me like this? I could have you thrown in prison for the rest of your life."

"You could. Put me in front of a firing squad if you wish. But as I'm sure Mr. Graves told you, I'm the only person who knows the full process for producing the antidote. Do anything but what I've asked, and you—and fourteen hundred other important people—will die."

Lochness stared at him for a long time. "Wirth, everyone has their price. What's yours? I can make you rich beyond your wildest dreams, set you up with the world's best research facility. Just produce the antidote. Or better yet, produce the antidote and let me control who gets it."

"Not interested. I've named my price, and the only way you or anyone else will get the antidote is when I, or a member of the team, injects it into you—after the multinational withdrawal from the Middle East. That's non-negotiable, Mr. President."

"Do you know what will happen there if everyone withdraws?"

"No, I don't. The region might blow itself to pieces. Or the people might decide they're tired of blowing themselves to pieces. Lines on a map drawn by France and England during World War I might get erased and new countries set up. They might trade their oil and whatever else they have to offer with the rest of the world, or they might not. They can't eat their oil. I don't think they'll do any worse managing their own affairs than the mess that's already been made. No more regime changes, no more nation building, no more interventions that never end, no more American kids flying home in coffins.

Whatever they decide, it will be their decisions, maybe their revolutions and wars. But it won't be you and your fellow megalomaniacs moving pieces on a chessboard."

"How much time do I have before we start dying?"

"About four months."

The president said nothing for an uncomfortably long time. "All right, I'll do what you're demanding. I don't have a choice, do I?"

"No, you don't. The antidote will require a booster every two years, so don't think that you and your partners in crime can do something cosmetic and then backslide into the same old idiocy."

"You're a real son of a bitch."

"Another thing: Carlos Valencia and his son and wife get released from wherever your goons are holding them. That happens today."

"They'll have to agree to keep quiet."

It would be a small compromise, well worth everything else he had won. "Okay. I'll leave it to the Valencias as to whether they agree to that."

"If there's nothing else, Wirth, we're done here." The president stood.

Ted stood and Lochness extended his hand. The hand of a ruthless killer.

"Shaking hands is how two parties who trust each other conclude and seal their deal. I don't trust you, Mr. President. This deal isn't sealed until the United States and the other countries leave."

⤙

Carlos Valencia read through the four pages of the government's nondisclosure agreement and picked up a pen. He had no idea why the government was letting him, Peter, and Anita go, but if agreeing to bury the Syria story was the price, so be it. They couldn't stay in prison, and Denise couldn't stay with the Sayers. He wouldn't do that to his family, make them First Amendment martyrs. He, Peter, and Anita signed nondisclosure agreements, and an hour later the entire family was back home.

CHAPTER 22

HISTORIC AGREEMENT

The secretary general of the United Nations stood before the General Assembly, convened for an extraordinary session and announcement.

"Distinguished heads of state, ambassadors to the United Nations, ladies and gentlemen, it is my pleasure to announce what may be the most important agreement ever reached under the auspices of the United Nations.

"Diplomatic teams and the heads of state of the United States, Russia, China, members of the European Union, members of the Cooperation Council for the Arab States of the Gulf, Turkey, Syria, Iraq, Iran, Afghanistan, Pakistan, Yemen, Lebanon, Jordan, Egypt, Libya, and Israel have agreed to withdraw their forces and armaments from all foreign nations in the Middle East and North Africa. Each country in those regions will be responsible for the affairs within in its own borders, but the agreement bans interference from foreign powers inside or outside of those regions. Any country that does interfere will be subject to extensive political, financial, and economic sanctions. This agreement in no way hinders trade, investment, tourism, cultural exchange, or any manner of peaceful intercourse between nations."

There was a smattering of applause, but mostly stunned silence.

"The Middle East and North Africa have become a cradle of violence and terror, of human desperation and misery..."

The secretary general's speech lasted over two hours. He reviewed the sad history of the region. There had been a meeting of the minds between President Lochness and Premier Roskolnikov: dramatic change was necessary. At a secret session, they had agreed to withdraw their forces and to persuade the other nations' leaders to do the same. Those leaders had agreed in remarkably short order. Left unsaid: they would have found it virtually impossible to resist the combined blandishments and threats of the United States and Russia. Diplomatic teams, working around the clock, drafted the historic agreement in world-record time.

The secretary general reviewed its provisions, particularly its enforcement mechanisms.

"This agreement offers the best—and for many, the first—hope they have ever known for peace and the only opportunity they have ever had for self-determination, a real voice in their own governance. I call on the members of these United Nations to ratify this unprecedented departure from business as usual. We must take a new road; let us boldly take the first step."

There was applause—polite, not thunderous—as the secretary general stepped away from the dais. He wiped sweat from his forehead. Was he taking ill? He had been told that it would be at least a month before he did so, but that margin gave him no comfort. There were assurances from the world's leaders that their military withdrawals would begin immediately, but those assurances gave him no comfort. His anxiety wouldn't diminish until after he had received the PHF antidote, and surely, as secretary general of the United Nations, he should be toward the front of the line.

$$\lambda$$

At the front of the line was President Lloyd L. Lochness. He stepped into a small conference room in the White House, one of two set up for the United States' high and mighty to secretly receive their antidotes. The media were fed a story about a summit of political, business, financial, and opinion leaders. The only members of the media who would know the true purpose of the summit were the media barons who were to receive the antidote. Linda was administering antidotes in the other conference room. Heather kept the procedure organized and on track. The other members of the team had fanned out across the globe. Elaborate precautions had been taken so that the antidote could not be confiscated and replicated.

"If you'll roll up your sleeve, Mr. President," Ted instructed.

Lochness rolled up his sleeve. Ted swabbed an area below his shoulder with an alcohol-soaked cotton ball and gave him his shot. He covered the bleeding hole with a gauze pad and put a Band-Aid over it.

"That's it, Mr. President." Ted glanced at a computer screen set up on the conference-room table.

"You know, the Middle East and North Africa will become hellholes. They'll make what they are today look like a Sunday picnic. That'll be on your head."

"Blow it out your ass, Mr. President. Send in Vice President Winslow."

⅄

Heather had seen Jill Yates's name on the list and wondered how Yates would act when it was her turn to receive the antidote. Her foundation, ostensibly devoted to improving the lot of the world's impoverished and downtrodden, had provided the springboard research for the government's evil perpetuity project. She had undoubtedly been complicit in the NIAR's expropriation of Ted's research, and she had received the PHF treatment. Heather made it a point to be present for Yates's shot. She expected shame, contrition, and embarrassment, or at the very least, sheepishness.

Yates smiled at Heather and Linda Chang as she entered the second conference room set up for administration of antidote. "Heather, so good to see you again." She turned to Linda. "And you're Ms. Chang?"

"Yes."

"I believe we met once at the foundation."

"We did."

"Well, let's get this over with. I've always hated shots." She sat down on the examination table and pushed up the sleeve of her silk blouse. Linda gave her the shot and covered the hole with gauze and a Band-Aid.

Yates pulled her sleeve over the Band-Aid and got off the table. "Thank you. Maybe we can get together for coffee the next time I'm in San Diego at the foundation."

"Ms. Yates," Heather said, "as soon as all this is over, I'm resigning from the foundation."

"I am, too," Linda said.

Yates raised her eyebrows. "I see. Well, sometimes life presents new opportunities, and we have to move on. There's no hard feelings on my part. Be sure to use me as a reference. Good luck to the both of you." She walked out of the conference room. Heather and Linda stared at each other, astounded.

⋏

Zach Kruger, the director of Centralized Intelligence, entered Ted's conference room and sat on the examination table.

"Mr. Kruger, before I give you your shot, would you answer a couple of questions?"

Kruger's expression indicated that Ted's questions would be a tedious waste of his time.

"That jet that flew into the dam. That wasn't a terrorist operation, was it? It was somehow set up by the government."

Kruger didn't answer.

"Were those people in the Syrian villages actually gassed and killed? You'll raise yourself a rung in hell if that was a simulated attack."

"Give me my shot."

"Your refusal to answer speaks volumes." Ted administered the shot, sticking the needle in Kruger's arm more forcefully than necessary. Kruger didn't wait for his Band-Aid and walked out of the room.

⋏

"If you'd like to sit on the examining table, Mr. Speaker," Linda said. She didn't exactly know why, but from the moment he entered the room, she had the impression that the Speaker of the House of Representatives was troubled, even distraught. It was his posture. His shoulders were slumped as if he were bearing a heavy load. She felt vaguely uncomfortable and wished Heather hadn't left the room.

"Is there any way you can arrange not to give me the antidote, Ms..."

"Chang. Linda Chang. If you don't get the antidote, you'll die. It's a terrible way to die."

"I know. It's what I deserve, going along with all this. I'll let you in on a secret, Ms. Chang. If this had worked as planned, Lochness was going to use PHF to ram through an amendment repealing the Twenty-Second Amendment."

"Which one is that?"

"It limits the president to two terms. There's no telling how far that bastard would have gone. It's easy enough in Washington to get dirt on people, to blackmail them, but imagine the leverage, promising the fountain of youth. And I went along with it. I sacrificed our soldiers...for me and a bunch of other bastards. Let me die, Ms. Chang."

"I can't. We're under strict orders from the president. Everyone has to receive the antidote."

"That's how Lochness thinks. Someone who wants to die has nothing to lose and might expose what's happened. If you've got to give me the shot, give me the shot." His voice dropped to a whisper. "Damned America."

Linda gave him his shot.

"Thank you," he said morosely, and left the room.

That evening, Speaker Portman drafted a lengthy e-mail that laid out all the details of the perpetuity project. He sent it to media outlets, then hung himself from a banister in his opulent townhouse. His e-mail was never published, and no mention of it was made in the many stories about his death. The stories said he was despondent about his failure to secure passage of a large increase in military funding.

CHAPTER 23

PEACE

The chairwoman of the Norwegian Noble Committee presented the cowinner of the Nobel Peace Prize, Russian premier Rodion Raskolnikov, with his diploma and gold medal. She then presented a diploma and gold medal to the cowinner and coarchitect of peace in the Middle East and North Africa, US president Lloyd L. Lochness. Oslo City Hall erupted in applause. The television camera scanned the audience, stopping at the Royal Family of Norway, seated at the front of the assemblage.

"Unless you want to listen to speeches from the Russian bastard and the American bastard, I'm going to turn it off," Ted said, reaching for the remote. He and Heather were watching their big-screen TV from their king-sized bed. They had moved into an apartment together.

"Go ahead. We have better things to do. By the way"—Heather's voice dropped to a whisper—"have you decided what you're going to put in those two-year booster shots?" Their paranoia about government surveillance had not subsided. They whispered when they communicated about sensitive subjects.

"Probably just saline solution and a harmless dye," he whispered back. "They'll never know it's not real. Keeps them honest. Keeps us alive."

"To think those two got the Nobel Peace Prize." Her voice returned to its normal volume. "They should give that prize to you."

Ted shook his head; he wanted no prizes.

The withdrawal from the Middle East and North Africa had defied the doomsayers' predictions. The region was no Shangri-La, but the foreign presences that had fueled much of its violence and terrorism were gone. Around the globe, fewer Muslims were blowing up, gunning down, or otherwise murdering innocents, although such horrors would probably never be completely eliminated. There would always be the Sunni-Shia schism, but there was talk of partitions—redrawing the lines on the map drawn by the French and English in World War I—to reflect sectarian realities. Responsible elements, builders rather than destroyers, were beginning the hard work of solving problems, addressing grievances, and binding wounds. Some of the region's "authoritarian" leaders were making noises about liberalization. One optimistic sign: refugee flows were reversing; more people were returning than leaving.

For that progress, halting and incomplete as it was, Ted would put up with the horseshit. The hypocrisy of the peace prizes. The lies. The propaganda dished out by the government and media. The knowledge that the powers that be were irretrievably corrupt and evil. His team's agreement to keep quiet. He would put up with the horseshit because absent the foreign powers who had contested it for centuries, the region had been given a chance to heal, its people a chance to live their lives as they saw fit. It might take generations, but hope had been resurrected where hope had long ago perished.

Perhaps Audrey Elkington and the other donors hadn't died in vain. Perhaps they had died for the cause for which they had given their lives: peace and freedom in lands that had never known those blessings.

ABOUT THE AUTHOR

Robert Gore graduated from UCLA, summa cum laude and phi beta kappa, with a double major in economics and political science. He received graduate degrees from UC Berkeley in business and law.

Gore traded bonds, was a partner, the director of the fixed-income division, and on the management committee for a Los Angeles-based securities firm. He appeared on television and radio programs as an expert on fixed-income securities.

After twenty-eight years in the securities industry, Gore retired to focus on his writing. He has previously published *The Gordian Knot*, a legal thriller, and *The Golden Pinnacle*, a historical novel. His articles and commentaries have been featured on a number of prominent websites.

Gore lives with his wife, son, and three cats in Albuquerque, New Mexico. He enjoys skiing, swimming, bowling, fishing, and mountain biking. For more information, he invites readers to visit his website, www.straighlinelogic.com.